I0784333

Praise

The Ten Commandments Reboot is a masterpiece of literary, creative, genius! An utterly hilarious satire on the Ten Commandments. With his laser sharpwit, Gershon Siegel offers deep insights on religion and our modern culture with its woes, adeptly weaving in solutions with his impeccably clear observations. Every page will leave you laughing, entertained, and informed—all done in such an engaging manner that even the serious readers (or religious scholars) will see the point. A veritable treasure trove that is wholeheartedly—and enthusiastically—recommended.

— **Sanjiv Manifest,** Cofounder, StillnessSpeaks.com

The Ten Commandments Reboot is a superb book, and I lingered long over its humor-spiced wisdom. I especially appreciate that it was cowritten by both God and Beelzebub, thus resolving conflicting absolutes that have buggered the minds of countless millions exposed to the Old Testament. I'm particularly happy with the way the book segues from the "Chosen People" to "everyone." Homo sapiens are the chosen species. This new interpretation of the Ten Commandments is on the mark, and the additional commandments work for me. This is a fine book to be mulled over vigorously as we pause at the edge of the abyss.

— **Jack Loeffler,** author of *A Pagan Polemic: Reflections on Nature, Consciousness and Anarchism* and *Adventures with Ed: A Portrait of Abbey*

Finally, and at what seems like the last possible moment, God has reengaged with humanity to offer us the full instruction manual we were always intended to have. Wisely eliciting the help of Beelzebub (who has been mercilessly slandered by history) in producing this manual, God is attempting to avert global disaster in the nick of time. *The Ten Commandments Reboot* not only offers us the full, uncondensed text of the Ten Commandments we think we know, but also five additional commandments that were always meant to be included, and which focus primarily on improving our emotional and inter-personal lives (don't be greedy, use your gifts, pay attention, live in joy, choose kindness). While one might argue that God could, perhaps, have gotten this done a lot sooner—because really, what else does God have to do with Infinite Time?—the correction is better late than never, and as a species, we can all benefit from these new and improved guidelines.

— **Jennifer Caplan,** author of
*Funny, You Don't Look Funny: Judaism and Humor from
The Silent Generation to Millennials*

Gershon Siegel rewrites the Commandments! It takes a lot of chutzpah and imagination to tackle a few thousand years of monotheistic culture and writing, and Siegel has the touch. Funny, irreverent, very Jewish. It's Mel Brooks meets Moses. And yet, after reading, you walk away with a sense that the authors of the Old Testament could've used some of Siegel's insight and biting humor. The ending is a bit of a well-considered warning to our current culture, but it is on point. My only concern is that Gershon seems a little obsessed with circumcision. Did something go wrong at his?

— **Hersch Wilson,** author of *Firefighter Zen: A Field
Guide for Thriving in Tough Times*

The Ten Commandments Reboot is a really valuable guide to living up to one's fullest potential. At the same time, Siegel's lighthearted satirical book provides a recipe for how all of us can be Heaven's cocreators that help to "awaken all humanity toward its upward evolutionary impulse." A short read, *Reboot* is well worth your time.

— **Bruce Berlin**, author of *Breaking Big Money's Grip on America*

Gershon exhibits a wry sense of humor and has a knack for fresh and unique delivery. While he's sometimes philosophically deep, much of his work is LOL funny, and some of his levity may cause the sensitive reader to blush. He has a real gift.

— **Michael S. Robinson, Sr.**, writes "Taking a Gander," a column for the *Salt Lake City Weekly*.

THE TEN
COMMANDMENTS
REBOOT

THE TEN COMMANDMENTS REBOOT

GERSHON SIEGEL

Permanent Press
Santa Fe, New Mexico

The Ten Commandments Reboot
Gershon Siegel
Copyright © 2025 by Gershon Siegel

No AI was used in writing this book.

ISBN, print: 979-8-9913136-0-5
ISBN, e-book: 979-8-9913136-1-2
LCCN: 2024917285

Permanent Press
Santa Fe, New Mexico

Editing by Melanie Mulhall, Dragonheart, www.TheDragonheart.com
Book design by Journey Bound Publishing

First Edition

Contents

Foreword

ALTHOUGH THE TEN COMMANDMENTS, AS given to Moses, are central to this book, this is not, by any means, a "Jewish" text. While these ten ancient statements, allegedly given by God, are sourced in Hebraic tradition, one might argue that the values and guidance enshrined within them undergird much of what passes for Western civilization. This book makes the case that the Ten Commandments, as we know them, are but a fraction of the divine guidance Heaven intended for all of humanity. If Moses had not redacted the overwhelming majority of Heaven's words, humanity would not now be facing an existential crisis—pretty much of its own making.

We say "pretty much" because, according to the following narrative, Heaven itself miscalculated several critical points in its planning of the Humankind Project. Revealed here for the first time is Heaven's intent in creating humanity as well as its own fractious debate over how best to help humanity fulfill that divine intent. *The Ten Commandments Reboot* makes clear that humanity was created to take on its share of managing the delicate life-sustaining systems of Mother Earth. That the Humankind Project seems to be going off the rails is the reason for this book. The postmodern rumors that God is dead and that humans are but a giant accident of biological evolution with no purpose, no meaning, and no higher calling are just that—rumors.

From the get-go, humanity has been hamstrung from fulfilling its destiny because of Heaven's own lack of foresight. In Heaven's attempt to make a species that would "spiritualize" physical reality, it failed to take into account the severe constraints of a physical universe based in dualism. When everything humans perceive comes in opposites, how can they not feel schizophrenic? This book purports to be Heaven's good faith attempt to take responsibility for its bad planning.

Herein, Heaven also admits to its naiveté in giving Moses a free hand in editing its original fifteen statements as he saw fit—even eliminating five of them altogether. This explains why so much of the original text of the Ten Commandments was never seen by the public. Appropriately enough, Heaven is using this opportunity to offer a heartfelt apology for allowing the first edition, as redacted by Moses, to be the only one familiar to us all.

In addition to restoring and updating the missing text from the Ten Commandments, there are, for the first time, five lost commandments. And although Moses did allow "Humanity's Quick Setup Guide for the Three Divine Gifts of Intelligent Awareness" to be made available to only a small, esoteric circle of priests and adepts, Heaven has chosen to also make that available to everyone reading this book.

The divine entities hovering around Mother Earth hope that in publishing the Commandments in its entirety, humanity will come to know its true upward spiraling evolutionary destiny which, you may be surprised to learn, has nothing to do with your next shrimp cocktail or credit rating.

Her Holiness the First Ko' Shure Deli Mama
Corner of 33rd Street and Broadway
New York, New York
2024

Preface

Dear Esteemed Member of the Mechanigencia,

Unless you are devoid of all conscience, ignoring a cry for help will come back to haunt you like a slice of forgotten camembert hiding in the back of your fridge. Should that plea come from a forever friend, you are inflicting a hurt only such a friend might forgive. How then, in spite of all my many misgivings, could I refuse just such a call from my oldest, most esteemed colleague? I could not, and this book is a testimony that I did not.

Over the millennia, my cocreator, buddy, and teammate has been known to you down there by such of names as "God," "Father Sun," "Allah," "First Cause," "Father Sky," "Jah," "Great Spirit," and even "Lord of Lords," which is over the top IMHO. Up here we mostly just call It "SOP," our affectionate nickname for "Source of Powers."

Now you can call It "Yahweh," "Elohim," or "Adonai." You can call It any of six dozen other names used throughout human history. But when SOP asks for help, you are wise to get your ass in gear and give it your all.

In my case, SOP's sudden request for help writing this book came as both a shock and a golden opportunity. To my great happiness, being of service to SOP in humanity's critical hour of need has given me a long awaited opportunity to clear the eons of lingering foul air between us. Sad to say, much of the blame for humanity's potential impending extinction has been laid, fairly or not, directly at my feet (which BTW, are not in the least cloven, although I do sometimes forget to trim my toenails).

The troubles between SOP and me started soon after humanity began its serious breeding on Mother Earth. Humans were still in their nomadic, hunter-gatherer phase, a time when a culture of organized cooperation within clans was slowly developing. Not coincidently, the trance inducing effects of drumming, chanting, and dancing were also being discovered.

But by far the biggest boost to early human transcendent awareness happened while they were pursuing the vast buffalo herds across the African savannahs. Always curious, these early hunters could hardly resist ingesting the plentiful, succulent fungi growing from fresh bovine droppings. Mere food gathering transformed into divine communion. Almost overnight, your ancestors' consciousness was catapulted above and beyond a simple instinctual push for survival.

Within just a couple of generations, feeble elders once left to die as unproductive burdens to the clan became honored keepers of tradition and wisdom. Except for times of severe drought, fighting for territory and resources among these groups nearly vanished. From my perspective, your species was moving toward the cocreative role Heaven had always intended humans to assume.

But as far as SOP was concerned, humanity's steady upward evolutionary path was proceeding too slowly. Habituated in its role as your Creator, SOP continued to micromanage what those of us in Heaven began calling SOP's Humankind Project. Famous for impatience, SOP became convinced that human numbers weren't growing fast enough.

At this point, SOP ordered Heaven's creation and maintenance team to engineer fertile plains in the paths of those tribes making their yearly nomadic cycles. Within three or four of these cycles, these fertile plains, offering reliable abundant food sources, became permanent settlements. SOP got just what it wanted: an accelerated pace of population growth.

Your species, which is often too clever for its own good, soon developed techniques such as fencing and irrigation that enhanced annual crop production. In no time at all, the nomadic hunting-gathering lifestyle was replaced by an agrarian one. Humankind's main problems quickly went from finding scarce food and game to protecting the growing surplus of grain from other species, particularly rodents.

Divisions in the population based on specialized labor began to appear. A priestly class of weather predictors who based their prognostications on stargazing emerged. Families devoted to building storage bins for crops forbade their sons and daughters from marrying into families who tilled the soil and grew the crops. Even within these classes, jealousy and infighting became normalized.

Happy with its planned population explosion, SOP took little notice of the troubling, unintended consequences. But many of us in Heaven became quite concerned, and a group of archangels elected me, as second-in-command, to tell SOP about humanity's divisive behaviors and what might be done about the problem.

Knowing this was a delicate situation, I casually approached SOP, nonchalantly offering a bit of friendly, if unsolicited, advice. I suggested that SOP take a long, overdue vacation from managing the Humankind Project. "Given that humanity's numbers have increased as they have, maybe it might be wise to allow it to develop on its own for a dozen or so millennia," I suggested. SOP then confided in me that after seven billion years, it was feeling creation burnout.

The next thing all of us in Heaven knew, SOP showed up with a duffel bag at a special meeting of archangels I had been assigned to arrange. "We (using the royal "we" as usual) have been hearing from other sources that there are some primo beaches on lovely planets in faraway galaxies that are perfect for renewing one's creative energies," SOP announced. "In our absence, we wish everyone here to do their part in keeping the Humankind Project on track. Until I return in eight or, at most, ten millennia, Beelzebub is in charge." And with that, SOP picked up its duffel bag and vanished.

As is said, the rest is history. When SOP returned from its nine-thousand-year vacation, humans were not faring very well. The hands-off humanity policy I had instigated in SOP's absence turned out to be a major flop. Except for a few scattered tribes still sticking with the old nomadic hunting-gathering ways, humanity's permanent settlements had become teeming cities of thousands—and often hundreds of thousands—of troubled souls. As we had seen early on, these cities had become centers of societal class division. They had also become vectors of disease, crime, human sacrifice, exploitation, and other innumerable forms of corruption.

So-called royal families ruling these cities kept busy by collecting taxes to support their lavish building projects and opulent lifestyles. They also created standing armies to conquer other cities. The priestly classes, instead of helping the "lower" classes pierce the veil hiding Heaven's divine intent, developed their own intention: amassing wealth and power. The Humankind Project had pretty much gone off the rails.

After hearing of humanity's inhumane behavior, SOP was, to say the least, angry with me. Earth's Humankind Project, with which I had been entrusted, was on a steep downward spiral. From then on, SOP barely spoke to me. So when SOP asked for my help with this book, I knew right away, in spite of all my reservations, that this was my chance to reconcile our once very close relationship. This collaborative effort marks a new era in our personal and professional relationship, and all in Heaven rejoice.

The serious mischief now metastasizing over your entire planet started with a simple wish on my part to help. But my mea culpa comes with a caveat. While I admit to a portion of the responsibility for humanity's undeniably unfortunate circumstances, in the name of objective justice, must I bear all of it? Or even half of it? SOP could have simply ignored me, not taken that extended vacation, and continued on in its merry micromanaging way.

Everyone in Heaven was always aware that when it came to Homo sapiens and Mother Earth, SOP had been exceedingly territorial. Why SOP didn't give up on humanity long ago has been a long running mystery to the heavenly hosts. From time to time, other promising species have caught much of Heaven's attention. The well researched, peer-reviewed report titled "Termites: Master Builders of Sustainability," by Archangel

Schmoozer, made a powerful argument against putting all of Heaven's evolutionary eggs in one basket. SOP politely accepted Schmoozer's signed copy, but everyone could tell it was going to sit on a shelf gathering stardust.

Ever since humankind invented the catapult, we in Heaven have sensed a kind of buyer's remorse souring SOP's attachment to humanity. Once upon a time, humanity and Mother Earth were SOP's favorite creations. But that was then. Now that there are quite a few unspoiled, pristine planets spinning smoothly right here in your galaxy ready to support abundant life—including Homo sapiens—who can blame SOP for developing a bit of a roving eye? From my perspective, SOP's recent flirtation with other planets portends a healthy development.

Following that German-engineered Jewish Holocaust, SOP sank into a denial stage as deep as the Grand Canyon and only now seems to be coming out of it. Not that that Holocaust was the first ever. Heaven has always been aware of light-skinned people's proclivity for wiping out whatever darker-skinned people they happened upon.

Heaven also knows that subsequent holocausts continue unabated. You have your Cambodian, Rwandan, Hutu, Uganda, Darfur, East Timor, Bambuti, and Guatemala genocides. And that one down in Myanmar. But it was that particular Jewish one that really kicked SOP in the kishkes. And now, watching the twice-chosen Jews abuse Palestinians as Jews themselves were once abused, it's all become too much.

As you are to learn, when it came to chosen peoples, the Hebrew tribes were not SOP's first choice. And after so many of them got involved with tax collecting, money lending, and managing hedge funds, the heavenly hosts began noticing something off in SOP's demeanor. Now, with Israel conducting its own ethnic cleansing, SOP has taken to wearing black and sitting shiva for all Jews supporting such unforgiving, deranged actions.

Even previous to that, SOP's covenant with the children of Abraham received a giant nail in its coffin when Freud's nephew, Edward Bernays, pretty much single-handedly invented the public relations industry. After so many Hebrews then rushed into the advertising business, SOP became visibly depressed. I remember once trying to cheer SOP up by joking that I could arrange a "special place" in my domain where Bernays' soul could burn for the rest of eternity. I think SOP thought I was serious. Although SOP will utter an occasional pun (the best ones being inadvertent), humor was never one of SOP's keenest senses.

I fear I may have wandered a bit from my purpose in providing this background and may even have gotten ahead of myself a bit. You may be wondering why SOP decided it was time for this expository volume. There is a contrast in the collective tone of Heaven between your current times and when we had just handed down the Ten Commandments through Saint Moses (who, as you will also learn, is a saint in name only). Taking a cue from SOP, nearly all my fellow archangels suddenly elevated expectations for all of humanity, not just for the Hebrews. You could say the heavenly hosts were floating on cloud nine. I kept my skepticism to myself. Who wants to drop a turd in the punch bowl?

Today, SOP's naive streak is not as wide as it was back then. Since that first truncated delivery of the Ten Commandments, thanks to Saint Moses, SOP's expectations for a humanity course correction are much lower. I suspect this book is an obligatory exercise aimed at relieving any residual remorse SOP still feels for the failing Humankind Project.

Even before the height of the Babylonian Era, Heaven has been watching in dismay at humanity's hapless slide down the evolutionary ladder. For reasons explained elsewhere, an unwillingness to make the required effort to climb back up is now pandemic among you. With few exceptions, each of your succeeding generations has become less inclined to realize its divine potential.

And thanks to Saint Moses, only small, isolated pockets of humanity are appreciating and using the divine gifts of being human. Instead of using your brilliant flexible thinking and self-awareness given only to Homo sapiens, your primary focus fixates on food, fashion, procreation, and social media. You are rapidly devolving. If not for the spacebar on your keyboard, your opposing thumbs would have become vestigial organs.

When SOP started blaming itself for humanity's evolutionary inertia, I knew I had to do something. SOP's self-recrimination got to be very unpleasant to be around. It started indulging in self-flagellation and wearing a hair shirt it never changed. Things got pretty ripe up here, if you smell what I'm stepping in. Heaven's usual calypso atmosphere, which had already been waning, became a dirge. None of the heavenly hosts felt like hosting anymore. Celestial Catering, Inc. even considered bankruptcy.

Since I was already on the outs with SOP and had little to lose, I once again stuck my nose where it didn't belong. I reminded SOP of my share of the responsibility for your ill-fated planet. I was hoping SOP might regain some perspective by realizing there was plenty of blame to go around—much of it coming, of course, from the arrogant, indulgent, sex-obsessed, suggestible, uncurious, ungrateful, unforgiving behavior of humanity itself.

This time, whispering in SOP's ear worked out way better than my original unsolicited extended vacation advice. SOP's whole demeanor changed, as if a sixteen-megaton bomb of remorse suddenly vanished. SOP stopped moping, finally changed its hair shirt, and got back to the work of creation—which was fortunate for Celestial Catering, Inc. The heavenly hosts started hosting once again, and it's been party time up here ever since. Limbo, limbo.

As far as SOP getting back into the work of creation, don't expect any divine intervention aimed at repairing the damage humanity has inflicted on itself and Mother Earth. SOP has given an oath that this book is a final attempt at micromanaging the Humankind Project. My advice to you is to be willing for the divine intention herein to guide your personal wills, both collectively and individually.

This book attempts to make amends for Heaven's mistakes with the Humankind Project. The ball is now in your hands. Try not to blow what looks to be your final chance.

Supreme Archangel Beelzebub
2024 (Earth Time)
This Side of the Galaxy

Introduction

My Dearest Children of the Humankind Project,

On behalf of Heaven, we wish to express our sincerest condolences to all of humanity for its most current existential crisis. We are sorry to inform you that this one is a real doozy, and the multiple calamities now facing you were not in Heaven's original plan. Our intention was to have humans become our cocreators and the mature managers of Mother Earth. Much of the responsibility for this failure results from the unlearned lessons prepared for humanity by Heaven.

Please know that Heaven had long ago prepared step-by-step detailed instructions needed for humanity's upward evolution in consciousness. Your tragedy begins with those instructions never being fully communicated. The missing parts to our meticulous human curriculum have proved disastrous to your species. Heaven now looks upon its failing Humankind Project with the deepest of regrets. Even worse, Mother Earth herself suffers mightily for having sustained you.

The Ten Commandments, as you have known them for over two thousand years, are but a snippet of the divine instructions Heaven had carefully prepared for the Humankind Project.

That even in their fragmented form these ten abbreviated statements still became, at least for a time, the organizing principle of Western Civilization is nothing short of miraculous. If only humanity had had access to Heaven's entire set of instructions, this, our last-ditch effort to supply them to you here, would be unnecessary.

Heaven's curriculum for its chosen people was designed with much care to teach humanity the proper behaviors for sustaining its upward evolutionary impulse. That humanity didn't learn these behaviors can all too easily be laid at humanity's feet. But this conclusion would be most unfair to humanity because Heaven failed to fully communicate its own lesson plans.

Much of humanity's impending demise lies with Heaven's creation and maintenance team becoming too lax in its mentoring role. So on behalf of Heaven, please accept our apology for the lack of guidance the children of the Humankind Project received—guidance they so desperately needed. Heaven has no real excuse for its dereliction of duty, which only deepens the collective sorrow it feels over humanity's arrested development.

As a result of Heaven's neglect, most of humanity is now missing the knowledge essential for achieving its divine destiny. Even worse, too many of you are now in outright denial that humanity even has a divine destiny. Heaven is not in the least proud of its contribution to humanity's sorry state of affairs.

This book is an attempt at a commandment reinstatement meant to guide humans back to their original divine destiny as Heaven's cocreator. Whether it is too little, too late to tug humanity back from the precipice on which it now teeters remains to be seen. Regardless, this is our effort to make amends, to correct the errors we have made with humanity, for which we feel remorse. Clearly, we were too casual and too hands-off in our management practices.

At this critical point in human history, making this information available now for as broad an audience as possible is the least Heaven can do. Though we have no delusions of saving everyone, this text might be considered a lifeboat of sorts, built to rescue some portion of panicked passengers who are not ready to go down with humanity's sinking ship.

In terms of human history on Mother Earth, 1623 BCE was both the worst of times and the best of times. On the one hand, Saint Moses had just completed his contractual agreement by helping Heaven deliver our then chosen people out of the land of Egypt—certainly a cause for celebration. On the other hand, our hernia never completely healed after parting the Sea of Reeds.

For the purpose of full disclosure, the reader should know that we are still feeling resentment toward Saint Moses. Had he not prevented us from sharing "Humanity's Quick Setup Guide for the Three Divine Gifts of Intelligent Awareness" with the masses as we had intended, most of you would have realized your divine natures by now. We are also certain that things would have turned out better for everyone had Saint Moses not edited our original fifteen statements down to the clipped, clichéd morsels now known to you as the Ten Commandments.

We knew at the time that asking humans to obey what might seem to be arbitrary rules without understanding the "why" was a setup for failure. In spite of that, we feel compelled to explain why Heaven granted Saint Moses final editorial powers. Doing so was yet another huge mistake on our part.

Please know that subsequently, we did send down five or six additional prophets tasked with explaining proper human behavior to correct our error. But because of humanity's afore-mentioned ignorance of proper behavior, there was a tendency to ignore or even persecute those prophets. If only the printing press had been invented earlier, we might have avoided those tragic deaths.

Even before the unfortunate Saint Jesus incident, we lined up a good half dozen more volunteer souls loung-ing in the reincarnation greenroom ready to echo his theme of universal love. Heaven rightly anticipated that the love-your-enemies-turn-the-other-cheek concept was going to be a very hard sell for most of you, so we geared up to hammer that moral home with these follow-up prophets. But when our bullpen of divine souls saw what happened to Saint Jesus, they opted to incarnate several millennia later as standup comics.

We would be remiss if we didn't inform you that this book is a coauthored effort. Without Supreme Archangel Beelzebub's prodigious help, it would not have the serious, yet mocking tone that is so appealing to current humanity's ironic sensibil-ities. After our eternity-long estrangement, we mention this to emphasize the huge significance of our reconciliation with Beelzebub. Among the heavenly hosts, our collaboration for this book is a very big deal.

So strong is our desire to buoy up humanity's sinking ship that we forced ourselves to listen to Archangel Beelzebub's pithy barbs of insight. He does have quite the sharp tongue, and one can only take so much criticism. Perhaps if we had been able to humble ourselves by asking for his help some time ago—like maybe before humanity's Industrial Revolution—your situation would not be so desperate.

As your history proves repeatedly, this kind of divine direct action is never successful for very long. Within a generation or two after Heaven offers humanity a course correction, our basic message is turned inside out, made into a new religion, or ignored altogether. No matter how simple and plain the language, critical elements in Heaven's directives become lost in translation.

This text may not bring the positive change to Mother Earth for which we are hoping. Given how close to the brink humanity now stands, your chances are dicey at best. We are somewhat shamefaced to admit that even if this book proves unhelpful in averting your impending disaster, it may at least lighten some of Heaven's heavy remorse for our past lack of supervision.

Sugarcoating humanity's situation is a disservice to all involved—to both those few humans continuing to shine a light on the path of evolution and to those of you posting selfies on Facebook or Instagram or whatever social media you use. Due to Heaven's goofs, way too many humans are blinded by the dark illusion of identification with their individual, separate selves. Getting humanity back onto its coevolutionary path will require the concerted effort of a good 10-15 percent of you using the compass of divine guidance implanted within each of you. Our hope is that this book will help you find your compass and follow the direction indicated.

In truth, there is little in this book that even the least informed among you do not already know. We are simply reminding you of certain instruments caked with dust in the tool kit each of you received at birth. Even a modicum of practice at brushing them off will bring you back in touch with your upward evolutionary impulse. More serious practice will be required, however, should you want to quiet those industrial-strength flushing sounds swirling across Mother Earth.

Offering you these potential course corrections reminds us of the hope Heaven felt when Saint Moses led those bewildered chosen people out of slavery. Hidden within humanity's current dire circumstances is a golden opportunity. As dark as it appears with all the seemingly impossible challenges now facing the continuation of your species, your individual possibilities are merely awaiting your awakening to them. You have what it takes. Please remember that the only sin is not using what is already yours.

Our comments are predicated on the assumption that humanity wants to survive. Heaven is crossing its collective fingers hoping that enough humans begin actualizing the material contained herein before collective karma catches up with them. If just 10-15 percent of humanity were to use the blessings Heaven has bestowed—such as of self-awareness, creativity, brilliant flexible thinking, intuitive knowing, remorse of conscience, compassion, forgiveness, and so forth—humanity on Mother Earth might avoid extinction. It couldn't hurt.

> In love, faith, and hope,
> Source of Powers, CEO
> 2024 (Earth Time)
> This Side of the Galaxy

"The Hebrews are saying that
You're a control freak."

1

What the Hell Was Heaven Thinking?

HEAVEN KNOWS MOST OF HUMANITY is hardly concerned with the Ten Commandments. If you're of a certain age, images from Cecile B. DeMille's 1956 film may float through your overstimulated mind. And for good reason. Ranking in the top ten of cinema's surreal moments, Charlton Heston's Moses is overcome by fear and awe, forced to turn away at the sight of a cartoon version of God's fiery finger chiseling Hebraic letters into stone. Sad to say, that campy Hollywood visual has left a deeper impression in the popular psyche than whatever morality humanity was to have received from those words over three millennia ago.

DeMille's depiction of Moses receiving Heaven's alleged words may very well be burned into humanity's imagination, but what really happened between Moses and Heaven's representative, while somewhat heated at times, tended more toward the tedious. Had DeMille stuck to the actual historical script that played out between the real Saint Moses and God, you would have thought you were watching *My Dinner with Andre* in slow motion.

The content of Heaven's original Ten Commandments would have taken up way more space than two teeny-weeny granite tablets could hold even if we had used ten-point type. Which, by association, reminds us of that movie scene in the Mel Brookes parody, *History of the World*, lampooning the DeMille/Heston depiction. Having received the commandments from Jehovah, Moses begins to announce that he is bringing fifteen commandments from God to the people but drops one of the three stone tablets on which they are written. Without skipping a beat, he tells them he has ten commandments. Even Beelzebub laughed at that one.

Just to show you how life imitates art, it just so happens that we did, in fact, present Saint Moses with fifteen commandments. Only we weren't calling them "commandments" when he first received them. "Commandment" is such a harsh term, and we tried to dissuade Moses from using it. But Moses had other ideas and hated so many of Heaven's *suggestions* that much of the text we gave him ended up on the cutting room floor (in keeping with the cinema parlance).

All kidding aside, we are not faulting Hollywood for hyping up the drama. Can you imagine the constant pressure Mr. DeMille was under from studio heads to produce a summer blockbuster? Still, with all the omniscience available to us, all of Heaven scratched its collective heads over how badly Edward G. Robinson was miscast.

Sorry. Let us put our pet cinema peeves aside and refocus on what we were actually thinking and intending for humankind with what has mistakenly been referred to as the Ten Commandments.

The Ten Commandments are a direct result of the Hebrews exiting from captivity in Egypt. Calling it a harrowing escape would be an understatement. You may recall how the parting of the Sea of Reeds was critical to their freedom. What is not widely known is that in addition to the thousands of pursuing Egyptian charioteers who drowned, a goodly number of Hebrew stragglers had their last gulp as well—mostly the sick, lame, and aged, as you would expect. One can only part a sea for so long. Not only did we get a hernia from it, we actually pulled a groin muscle.

What with all the trauma, many of the Hebrew survivors were confused, some even suffering from what might be called PTSD in today's terms. When you combine seven generations living as slaves on top of a very urgent exodus, dislocating them from the only home they had ever known, you can understand how the Hebrews lost their moral compass. They were a shadow of the chosen people previous to their time in Egypt. Both Saint Moses and the heavenly hosts agreed that a thorough revising of the original covenant made with them was necessary. What Heaven and Moses could not agree on were many crucial details we wanted in the new covenant.

We conferred with Archangel Gabriel and had him draft a kind of "Chosen People Covenant 2.0" that would consist of two documents. Of necessity, this version was a much more thorough document than the first one made with Abraham. In that original iteration, you may remember there was a simple circumcision clause imposed on each male child. Credit is due Archangel Shlong for coming up with that clever provision, which served two important functions. The sacrifice of snipping off foreskin brings real gravitas in being a chosen person. And at the same time, it helps to hold the Hebrews back from becoming too braggadocio, if you get my meaning.

In accepting our covenant, Abraham also understood that Heaven expected his tribe to be a righteous example for the goyim by always aspiring in thought, word, and action to live up to the human potential. And of course, in exchange for setting a righteous example, Heaven was to grant the Hebrews guidance and protection. But those were simpler times.

Subsequent to the exodus, Heaven needed humanity to have a much deeper understanding of what we expected from it. So we instructed Gabriel to create an instruction manual for humanity that would explain the inner workings of the human bio-machine. Titled, "Humanity's Quick Setup Guide for the Three Divine Gifts of Intelligent Awareness" ("the guide" for short), it was composed so humanity could develop the necessary capacities for becoming Heaven's cocreator.

After drafting the manual, Gabriel churned out a second document containing a list of specific behaviors intended to keep the chosen people worthy of that moniker. Included in this document were the reasons underlying these specific behaviors. Originally called *The Thirty Hebrew Edicts*, Heaven's editorial board complained it contained too much micromanaging. And rather than naming a particular group, we wanted a more generic title inviting all of humanity. Gabriel came back with *The Fifteen Statements*, the draft that we eventually presented to Saint Moses.

By far, the guide was the more important of the two documents. Without a knowledge of how to use the three divine gifts, humanity could not be expected to fully implement one or two mandates, let alone fifteen. Tragically, the guide was never delivered to the general public because Saint Moses withheld it.

Besides keeping the guide secreted away from the bulk of humanity, Saint Moses insisted on edits to *The Fifteen Statements*. He even went so far as to eliminate five of them altogether, which is how they came to be called the Ten Commandments. Saint Moses got his way because of certain editorial conditions we had foolishly allowed him. Being who we are, we have had little practice at compromise. The art of negotiation is not our forte.

Saint Moses contended that after so many generations of living as slaves, a newly freed people needed clear, barebones moral instruction. He insisted that "statements" was too weak a word. "Furthermore," he concluded, "the Hebrews have lost touch with exercising their free will, let alone a will that is divinely guided. They need solid laws to give them a sense of certainty. They need very simple, straightforward command-ments. Just tell them what to do and what not to do in no uncertain terms."

We could understand the need for simple and straight-forward, but who likes to be told what to do and what not to do? From our experience, certainly not the Hebrews. And those Kohanim and Levites? Forget about it. We were willing to compromise with *The Ten Suggestions*, but once again, Moses was insistent, so our suggestions aimed at stabilizing an entire nation of newly freed, not to mention traumatized, former stone quarry slaves came to be known to the world as "commandments."

Having to endure Saint Moses's extremely heavy-handed editing was humiliating. As you will see, his style of brevity was no-nonsense to the point of terse. Which is not to say that we did not need editing. Every writer needs a good editor, and we will be the first to admit that many of Moses's changes proved helpful. He knows how to be concise, while we tend to give more context than is sometimes necessary. Such is the burden of omniscience.

And speaking of editors, as alluded to above, we have enough self-awareness to know that we cannot lay all the responsibility for our previous miscommunications solely on humanity's lack of curiosity—nor on its inability to make sustained efforts at understanding. Some of our past misunderstandings with humanity lie with us.

Our tendency for excessive contextualizing can often result in giving too complex a picture for average human comprehension. Honing down our multifaceted perspective to a single-pointed message appropriate for the intended recipient has always been our challenge. That's why we called on Supreme Archangel Beelzebub to coauthor this project. Crafty beyond measure and conversant with the cynical attitude so pervasive in these times, we believe he has the language skills necessary for penetrating even the most compromised of human psyches.

Before giving you the repaired Ten Commandments, you need to become more than familiar with the material offered in the guide, which Heaven intended as a primer for all humans. Unfortunately, due to Saint Moses's insistence, the guide has only been available to a very small circle of humanity. In it are critical instructions for a complete understanding of the Ten Commandments.

Be advised, these are the Ten Commandments before they were heavily redacted by Saint Moses and after Archangel Beelzebub helped recontextualize them. We're both pleased with and grateful for how Beelzebub has kept the general intent of our original counsel while making it more accessible for the modern audience.

Be warned that Beelzebub also added his own brand of humor, which we often find overly sarcastic. But then, everyone has their shadow side, and given that Beelzebub *is* our shadow side, what did we expect from our evil twin?

Even with Beelzebub's prodigious knowledge of humanity's current schizoid state, there is no guarantee that our current collaboration will have the desired salubrious impact for which we hope. Let's face it, we're a bit late in the game, and humanity has demonstrated such poor management skills that Mother Earth is quickly losing her ability to sustain anything other than viruses. Not that we have anything against viruses.

Looking back at our original suggestions in the form of statements, it is embarrassing to see how defensive we were feeling at the time. Perhaps we were still beating ourselves up about leaving humanity to pretty much fend for itself soon after the creation. But in our defense, remember that we set you up in paradise—literally. We had not counted on how tempting that serpent was or the amount of greed contained in the human heart. All we asked of you was to leave alone the fruit of one lousy tree out of millions. But *no*!

In publishing these, our unabridged, Ten Commandments, as well as the five lost commandments, Heaven is crossing its collective fingers for the transformation of Homo sapiens to finally be worthy of their self-assumed name, "Wise Humans." But as has been alluded to, humanity is at the bottom of the ninth inning with no runs and no batters on. Time to step up to the plate.

2

Why a Chosen People in the First Place?

FOR A VARIETY OF COMPELLING reasons and in spite of a multitude of red flags, the heavenly hosts decided on creating a so-called "chosen" people. Almost a half dozen millennia have passed since granting one particular population special favors, and we have never heard the end of it. To this day, there are still many among you who believe this action to be Heaven's most ill-considered. Even a few archangels, as well as Beelzebub himself, fall into that camp.

Having observed the human animal for hundreds of thousands of years, we were quite aware of their curious tendency toward disunion, disruption, and disagreement. As far as Heaven was concerned, such behavior was counterproductive to the purpose for which humanity was created, so we took pains to avoid even the perception that Heaven blessed some among you but not others. Heaven had a policy of not intervening with humans—until we fabricated the concept of the chosen people.

There were minor exceptions to our nonintervention approach. Say there was a drought in a particular region with massive crop failures and many humans dying of thirst. We might have created just enough rain to help alleviate the situation. Or maybe there was a famine in one area and too many of the young were starving. Heaven might have nudged a herd of gazelle or buffalo to shift its usual migratory path into the affected district. We are not immune to compassion, but our involvement was kept at a minimum.

But at this one particular moment, with the Humankind Project on the brink of total failure for yet a second time, expediency took precedence over forethought. Fully aware that we were likely infecting humanity with the troublesome separation virus for generations to come, Heaven ignored its own best practices and made a bargain with a quirky little tribal band of sheep and goat herders. This was not a deal that Heaven took lightly.

Please understand that Heaven's love falls equally on every single being throughout all creation. No one need ever think, act, or feel that they are better or less than anyone else. To know this wholeheartedly is, in fact, one of the underlying lessons every human is born to learn—no matter their caste, socio-economic stratum, race, or gender. No one person or group of people is more special than any other. Period. End of story.

The whole point of seeding Mother Earth with Homo sapiens was to have them cooperate to the point of eventually taking over the planet's proper management. To preserve whatever little progress had been made in that direction, Heaven decided that divine intervention was necessary. Such was the case nearly six thousand years ago when most of humanity had forgotten, for yet a second time, its sacred evolutionary impulse. This second falling led Heaven to consider taking a very different tact than the one we'd taken the first time, twelve or so millennia earlier.

That first fall was like receiving a kick in the kishkes with spiked steel-toed boots. Heaven had watched in horror at the quickly growing numbers of humankind acting in ways not at all kind. The sight of so much divine potential being wasted on so many human souls was so disappointing that the heavenly hosts, with the exception of Archangel Beelzebub, went into mourning. For Beelzebub, this was an "I told you so" moment.

Way back then, it seemed prudent to assemble what we called the First Congress of Archangels to address humanity's first fall. You would have thought it was a funeral, which, in a way, it was. We unanimously voted to drown most every human on the planet. This was a result of accepting Archangel Brutus's proposal to start the Humankind Project over by wiping out the vast majority of them. Brutus's idea was to fill a fleet of arks with a couple of thousand decent enough folk ready to reboot Mother Earth's Homo sapiens experiment in conscious cocreation.

Beelzebub had a good laugh. It turned out there were barely enough righteous humans to fill even one ark, let alone a fleet. And even then, there was still enough room left over on that one vessel to fit elephants, giraffes, zebras, lions, tigers, bears—you name it. We're talking a real zoo. Maybe you read about it or have seen depictions? Artists of all kinds seem to love that image.

After humanity's first fall caused Heaven to take such drastic action, you can imagine our distress when the human experiment went south yet a second time. So the Second Congress of

Archangels was convened to ponder the appropriate action. A few of the rash among us with short memories urged revisiting the ark/flood solution. Those of us with cooler heads believed we could come up with a less drastic, more creative, more humane alternative. Plus, after that first flood, it had taken thousands of years for a viable human population to become established again. Widespread mold allergies and pink eye also gave us pause.

Archangel Mazel Tov suggested a faster, less painful way to restart the planet's people component. Rather than beginning the human experiment all over again from scratch, Mazel Tov asserted, "We could recruit a dozen or so nomadic tribes who still remember their evolutionary potential and live according to the laws of Heaven. Such a group would serve as an example for that portion of humanity still mired in the ways of murderous, pagan barbarians."

"Even if you could find two dozen righteous tribes," countered Archangel Nebbish, "how are you going to get them to agree to act as an example for the mass of devolved humanity? Whatever group you get to parade around as Mother Earth's goody-two-sandals will more likely be persecuted than imitated."

"This is why we recruit desert nomads," insisted Mazel Tov. "First of all, you should know that I've been watching a particular group scratching out a living in the desert. They're a very tough bunch. Surviving for nearly a thousand years in the harshest of conditions is no picnic. Their total reliance on each other has helped them retain the 'kind' in humankind. They may be a little arrogant, but they're a tight-knit group and know the strength of unity. They're also primed to worship an invisible spirit, for they forbid any of their members to fashion idols."

Mazel Tov paused for a moment to let what he'd said be considered. Then he continued with the kicker. "Secondly, we make these tribes an offer they can't refuse. We grant them a solemn covenant. Heaven showers blessings and protection upon them in exchange for their agreement to live as exemplars of evolutionary potential for all of humanity, yada yada. By living according to the word of the One True God and spreading it to those who have forgotten it, we guarantee that they, as well as their flocks of sheep and goats, will increase and multiply. How could the barbarians not take notice?"

"Oh, the barbarians will take notice, all right, Mazel Tov," replied the famously cynical Nebbish. "They will also be taking lots of sheep, goats, and whatever else your precious nomads manage to increase and multiply. And that will be the end of your righteous tribes."

Mazel Tov shook his head in frustration. "You're such a naysayer, Nebbish. Remember, nomads are very tough. And to make sure they can keep the barbarians at bay, we stipulate in the covenant that this 'special' tribe will have a permanent piece of land with defensible borders on which to settle. You think those tired nomads are going to turn their noses up at having their own nation?"

"And where will you find this bit of land with defensible borders?" asked Nebbish.

Archangel Mensch finally spoke up. "Stop being such a pill, Nebbish. It's so easy to criticize. Choosing a piece of land is much easier that choosing a people. How many generations of Amorites, Hittites, Perizzites, Hivites, Girgashites, and Jebusites have fought over that narrow slice of barren land next to the

Red Sea? They should have made the deserts of Canaan bloom by now. If these nomadic tribes are as tough as Archangel Mazel Tov says they are, how hard can it be to help them drive out those bickering Canaanites?"

How long and how hard the heavenly hosts have come to rue Archangel Mensch's words! Who knew that when we created the Law of Hazard, Heaven itself would be as subject to it as the mice and men springing from our divine loins? (Ask not why Heaven created the Law of Hazard. Beelzebub thought Humanity would be more grateful, and it seemed like a good idea at the time.)

Who knew the original covenant with Abraham would generate so many problems and so much confusion for all parties concerned? Who knew how attached those Canaanites and their cousins were to that narrow slice of barren land next to the Red Sea?

In defense of Heaven's choice of a promised land, we did consider other options. As far as what territory we were going to offer this yet-to-be-named chosen people, Archangel Meshuggah suggested using what is now called Utah. And he made a good case as to why it would be less controversial than Canaan, pointing out that it was pretty much uninhabited. The Utes had yet to settle there and the Mormons were thousands of years away from displacing the Utes.

"Whatever sand dune wandering nomads we pick as the chosen people," said Meshuggah, making finger air quotes around "the chosen people," "they are never going to know the difference. Seen one desert, seen them all."

We discussed the merits of Archangel Meshuggah's proposal, but in the end, we opted for the shorter, easier play. We convinced ourselves that moving a passel of tribes with their camels, sheep, and goats to the other side of the planet was going to be a logistical nightmare.

And as Archangel Alter Kocker pointed out, "If we intend for this chosen people to rekindle humanity's memories of its sacred duties, why put them in the middle of an uninhabited desert? Who, exactly, are they going to influence?"

Alter Kocker has always been quick to state the obvious, but if we had known how crazy long those Canaanites and their cousins were going to stay pissed off after being driven from their camel-stomping grounds, we might have considered Meshuggah's Utah proposal more seriously. And so it was that the Second Congress of Archangels adopted the chosen people option over a second worldwide drenching. On top of that and ultimately adding to the controversy, the Second Congress of Archangels also adopted the promised land covenant clause.

As predicted by Archangel Mensch, picking a promised land was the easy part. Choosing the people to put on said land was a bit more complicated. Archangel Mazel Tov was already lobbying for a group of nomadic Hebrews wandering around the Sinai Desert. Archangel Putz was doing the same for a large Bedouin group in the North of Africa. We, on the other hand, had our own ideas about a chosen people that would have made the promised land clause moot.

Rather than telling the group our thoughts on the matter, we motioned for a recess, knowing this discussion was likely to become quite heated. Deciding which people to choose for reestablishing humanity's evolutionary sacred being impulse was serious, not to mention a tedious business. Archangel Nosher, whose hunger pangs could be heard throughout the congress, seconded our motion. It passed almost unanimously, except for Beelzebub, who delights in watching the enduring stress of others.

But apart from knowing the discussion could become heated, we also knew that heated or not, it would have been a pointless discussion because we had already decided who the chosen people would be. You might call it a backroom deal. The democracy of the congress was all well and good, but sometimes to move forward in a timely manner, we need to forego taking the time to achieve consensus and just take matters into our own hands. Sad to say, in this particular case, doing so showed us how we're sometimes too clever for our own good.

3

Choosing the Hebrews the First Time

As much as we have wished for direct divine communication with humanity, with few exceptions, whenever face-to-face contact has been attempted, whether through visions, dreams, psychic readings, or what have you, our message gets badly mangled. Something always gets lost in translation. The main cause is that outside the earthly realm, reality is multidimensional, while humans dwell in three dimensions.

On a number of occasions, we've tried using human channels, but finding a personality who can refrain from embellishing our message is as rare as a chicken with lips. The Oracle of Delphi did pretty well for a short time, but then she let her celebrity status go to her head. We did have some success with the I Ching in the East and Ouija boards in the West when they were in vogue. But now everybody wants to consult with tarot decks, which allow far too much room for biased interpretation.

One thing we learned from Saint Moses about getting our point across to humans is to use simple, straightforward language. Homo sapiens are such a literal-minded bunch that analogies and metaphors tend to muddy the water, as it were. And parables can be so confusing. Just ask Saint Jesus.

In addition to sticking to simple language, over the centuries on those occasions when a person or a people really needed to hear our message, we learned a little trick from Beelzebub that fools the human psyche into a maximum state of receptivity. Timing is crucial, of course, and since we created time, we're usually pretty good at timing.

Let's say we're trying to drop some critical message on a person who needs to hear it but who is not the least bit interested or ready to hear it. What we do is pretend to be speaking to someone else while at the same moment letting the person we intend for the message in on the communication. Suddenly they become all ears and we've gotten our message through. What was once a message we knew they didn't really want to hear becomes magically cloaked in the false glamour of privileged information. Millions and millions of neurons in the person's brain become excited. Sleepy old synapses begin lighting up like a fireworks climax on the Fourth of July.

But just our luck, at this most important inflection point of trying to secure the chosen people, our little ruse at projecting a clear message to the right recipient went awry. The Law of Hazard bit us in the ass, which is very disconcerting since, along with time, we also created the Law of Hazard. (It was actually Beelzebub's idea, BTW.)

No doubt we're stepping on a few toes, but it's no secret that the Hebrews were not our first draft pick. First of all, they were a tiny population of nomads with no political clout whatsoever. As Archangel Mazel Tov pointed out, the Hebrews were not engaging in idolatry, but a nagging gut feeling told us they were not as receptive to Heaven's ways as one would want in a chosen people.

The Middle East's ongoing troubles between Arabs and Jews has proven our intuition correct. On more than one occasion, we nearly gave up on them altogether. And now, with Israel's latest ethnic cleansing efforts of its occupied territories, we're revoking our covenant. You heard it here first. This isn't the first time we've been disgusted with the Hebrew's stiff-necked behavior. We've even gone on record venting our frustration numerous times (See Exodus 33:3, Deuteronomy 9:13, Nehemiah 9:16, and Acts 7:51).

Admittedly, Mazel Tov's idea of using a feisty bunch of tight-knit desert nomads to reinstate the evolutionary impulse throughout humanity had some merit. But from a purely political perspective, the Babylonians, our personal first choice, were in a much stronger position to quickly influence the barbarian world.

Babylon was already an up-and-coming empire with a large, pretty sophisticated, settled population. True, it had more than twenty gods enmeshed in its mythology, so the idolatry issue would have proved contentious. But word on the street was that the average Babylonian was sick and tired of having to sacrifice burnt offerings to the likes of Apsu, Mummu, Kingu, and Nabu, to name a few.

The challenge of convincing Babylon to give up its multi-idol worshiping ways in exchange for the one invisible God concept would have been steep. But the whole mess created by the promised land clause would have been worth it. We were also convinced that an already established nation would spread our message with a great deal of efficiency. Remember, this was way before social media, when advertising was strictly word of mouth.

But here is where we screwed up big time. Instead of directly notifying Hammurabi, King of Babylonia, that his people were being tapped as our chosen ones, we stupidly pretended that our message was meant for Abraham, now known to you as the patriarch. Talk about bad timing. It turned out Hammurabi was caught up in some palace intrigue and never even overheard our message.

Abraham, hearing Heaven was in the market for a chosen people, insisted we consider his sad little collection of wandering tribes. It was all we could do to not laugh in his face. But oy, what a persistent pest Abraham turned out to be! He wouldn't let go, insisting that he and his people were ready to give up any hint of idolatry and follow our laws to the letter.

Now here is where we really schtupped the pooch. Believe us, we honestly tried to discourage Abraham. We knew that he and Sarah were into their nineties when they finally had their first child. We thought we could put him off by demanding that he kill his young son, Isaac, as a show of good faith. We figured Sarah was never going to let Abraham go through with such an outrageous demand.

Goes to show you the dangers of assumptions. To our horror, without even conferring with Sarah, Abraham grabbed his son and a knife and dragged him to the place of sacrifice. We're pretty sure he would have slit Issac's throat then and there had we not intervened. We knew Sarah was never going to let us hear the end of it. Maybe it was a bluff on Abraham's part, but the Law of Hazard was already eating our shorts and we couldn't chance it.

With much trepidation, we made our covenant with Abraham and his bloodline. But to show Abraham that becoming our chosen people was serious business, we inserted the circumcision stipulation. That was almost a deal-breaker, but when we dangled the promised land clause, Abraham dropped his objections on the condition that any male over the age of seventy be exempt from circumcision. We understood where he was coming from and agreed.

Abraham was quite happy with the covenant he'd managed to negotiate. In gaining our eternal protection for his people—not to mention a piece of land to call their own—all we wanted was a smidgen of Isaac's foreskin. Isaac, who must have been thirteen at the time, was less than thrilled. And we were less than thrilled at the prospect of explaining our unilateral action to our minions.

But here is the funny part. While we were going behind the backs of a host of archangels with our failed attempt to secure the Babylonians as the chosen people, Archangel Mazel Tov lobbied tirelessly and convinced a majority of his fellow archangels to vote for the Hebrews.

Soon after reconvening, the congress voted on which people would be living on the land that Heaven had already picked. Conveniently for us, the Hebrews won in a landslide over the Bedouins. After the vote, we graciously offered to contact the patriarch, Abraham, to make him an offer he would not refuse.

Except for Beelzebub, who's privy to every little thing we have ever done (or not done), none of the archangels were the wiser. The Congress of Archangels could continue believing in their delusion of democracy, and we were spared the embarrassment over our backfired trick with Hammurabi. Sometimes things work out in spite of the Law of Hazard.

4

Why the Hebrews a Second Time and Why Moses?

AND THEN AGAIN, AS THE Law of Hazard indicates, sometimes things just don't work out. In a mere thousand years or so after choosing the Hebrews to help actualize humanity's needed course correction, once again, too many Homo sapiens were failing to live up to their potential. But we can't blame it all on the Hebrews, even though much of their subsequent behavior has been less than helpful in raising human consciousness.

We do not like to be the kind of creator who says, "We told you so," but our initial resistance to choosing the Hebrews has been justified more than once. That being said, we admit that Abraham and most of his tribe did the chosen people pretty well—at least for the first ten or so centuries.

One has to remember that ancient Israel's conquering, killing, and enslaving happened well before our commandment forbidding murder. And even during their Egyptian enslavement, they held fast to the circumcision clause, which in reality was just an afterthought on our part. It's not like we needed the foreskins. We weren't collecting them. That would have been way too perverted.

And as an aside, you can imagine our disgust when Archangel Shlong, one of Heaven's most entrepreneurial archangels, opened up Café Divine Penis Envy, featuring fried foreskin with a side of curry yogurt dipping sauce. The very thought sickens us, and to this day we swear we have never tried one. Beelzebub did try to tempt us once, claiming that if we closed our eyes, we would think we were eating calamari.

Anyway, like we were saying, for a good ten or so centuries, the Hebrews set a good enough example for the rest of humanity that we were beginning to see an average level of consciousness elevation percolating throughout that region's general population. Which was, after all, the whole point of creating a chosen people. As a result, under our divine protection, the Hebrews grew in strength and numbers right along with their herds.

But with the Hebrews' physical success, a certain arrogance and greed began to arise. We noticed a number of them pushing beyond the original boundaries of the promised land. A few of the more aggressive among them, particularly those of the Naphtali, Dan, and Net'n Yahoo tribes, began proclaiming what they called settlements beyond the original agreed borders. Sound familiar?

Heaven ended up letting a handful of those incursions into neighboring territories slide with Archangel Mazel Tov rationalizing their behavior with the now famous question,

"When it comes to sand dunes as far as the eye can see, what is one or two hectares here or there?"

Everyone knew the Hebrews were occupying territories not included in our original covenant with Abraham. Set boundaries were crossed, plain and simple. We were very disappointed with our chosen people and called an informal assembly of archangels to discuss the matter.

Archangel Mazel Tov pointed out that the Hebrew encroachment was a learned behavior. "Heaven itself does the very same thing," he thundered, "but when Heaven does it, we call it divine intervention. Should the child be punished by imitating the behavior of its parent? Is Heaven going to tell the Hebrews, 'Do what I say, not what I do?'"

Needless to say, many of us were not at all convinced by Mazel Tov's strained rhetoric, but it did convince enough of the assembly that ignoring Israel's "little" transgressions would be the best policy. "After all, we do want to see the Hebrews continue to prosper, don't we?" Mazel Tov said, looking straight at us.

What Mazel Tov's argument completely ignored was that in the scheme of Heaven's plan, divine intervention is a short-term affair that soon disappears like smoke. But when humans ignore the sacred covenant clauses, serious long-term consequences are the result. Where the Hebrews were concerned, the encroaching behavior on their neighbor's territory was unequivocally wrong, and it was asking for trouble.

Why we let them get away with it for so long, Heaven knows. We would blame Mazel Tov and his silver-plated tongue, but "blame" is a dirty word up here, so we let the assembly's majority vote in favor of allowing Israel's illegal behavior stand.

We should have known Israel's behavior was a prelude of what was likely to come and nipped it in the bud. But we didn't, and sure enough, in no time at all, the Tribe of Naphtali conspired with the Dan and Net'n Yahoo tribes to sell the other ten tribes into Egyptian slavery. That's when the whole chosen people project really went south, literally. Whatever progress was made in raising the average barbarian's consciousness during those first thousand years as a chosen people became bubkes.

So why did we pick the Hebrews yet a second time to be the chosen people? This time, it wasn't the Hebrews' eternal lobbyist, Archangel Mazel Tov, but, much to our chagrin, it was Beelzebub who came to their defense.

We believe there was a growing number of archangels ready to go with another group of people. By that time, the Babylonian Empire had fallen on hard times and many of us figured they'd be very receptive to the idea. And the Sumerian Empire was enjoying a renaissance, so we considered them. We even considered the Assyrians, but they were not really viable candidates because they were still acting out their centuries-long brutal behavior. Even so, we were not without choices.

But Heaven needed to act quickly, so we called the Third Conference of Archangels for the express purpose of reviewing the whole chosen people debacle. A debate quickly ensued between Archangels Mazel Tov and Putz. Mazel Tov insisted that we give the Hebrews a second chance, and Putz claimed that had we gone with his Bedouin tribe, we would not be having this discussion. Archangel Kvetch tried throwing cold water on the whole idea, ranting that we should flood the planet a second time and start the whole Humankind Project over from scratch.

To everyone's surprise, because he so seldom gives his opinion in public, Beelzebub took the floor and addressed the group. "As you know, I'm an entity of few words. Generally, I'm inclined to let events play themselves out as they will. But in this case, I feel compelled to share my thoughts. For too long, Heaven has taken it upon itself to intervene in humanity's affairs. We have become intrusive parents to our charges. We have failed to allow them to mature on their own terms.

"If Homo sapiens are to grow into the proper cocreators we expect them to be, they must be given a chance to help themselves. How many millennia are we going to treat them like our playthings, drowning them or propping them up whenever we believe they're going in the wrong direction?"

Springing from his bench like some crazed coked-up frog, Archangel Kvetch shrieked, "That was exactly my point!"

"Oh shut up, Kvetch!" Beelzebub fired back. "You should know better than to interrupt me. How the hell did you ever make it to archangel status anyway?"

Kvetch turned a bright shade of red at the rebuke and immediately sat back down. A reprimand by one such as Supreme Archangel Beelzebub gives serious pause.

"As I was saying, if we continue treating Homo sapiens like children, they will remain as children. We need to include them in deciding their own destiny. Instead of picking a whole other people as exemplars for the rest of the barbarian population and hoping for the best, I propose we pick one outstanding leader who can team with us to help humanity fulfill its evolutionary potential."

A hush fell over the congress as everyone waited to hear more about Beelzebub's unprecedented proposal.

"I have found just such a leader," he finally said.

An excited buzz wafted through the congress.

"Many of you may not know that I have been observing the Egyptian situation ever since the bulk of Hebrews became slaves. In recent times, the leaders of Egypt have become quite concerned over what they now call the 'Hebrew problem.' Due largely to Heaven's original covenant with Abraham, the Hebrews continued to multiply, even under slavery. Pharaoh Seti became so paranoid of a slave rebellion, he ordered the slaying of all Hebrew newborn males. As you can imagine, the Pharaoh's action created quite the panic among the slave population.

"One desperate Hebrew mother, Jochebed by name, managed an escape for her infant son by cleverly floating him onto the River Nile near to where the pharaoh's daughter took her daily ablutions. Jochebed's hope was that the daughter would take pity on the helpless child, rescue him from the river, and raise him in the Pharaoh's household. Unlikely though it was, Jochebed's plan worked in a most miraculous way.

"Living as a prince in the Pharaoh's household, this fugitive Hebrew named Moses was given all the privileges due his royal status. Moses endeared himself to the whole of the Pharaoh's court. Seti was especially grateful when Moses, in his job as the palace's communications director, helped keep Seti's approval ratings somewhere in the high 70 percent range. This was no easy task given how the Pharaoh's agents routinely went about brutally collecting taxes.

"But Moses eventually lost favor in the Pharaoh's court after killing a number of Egyptian taskmasters who were diehard slave abusers. Threatened with death, he fled to Midian, where he remains in exile to this day, tending his father-in-law's sheep. He is now eighty years old, and from what I've seen, he has enough experience, grit, and charisma under his tunic to lead the Hebrews out of slavery. It is my belief that once back in the promised land after wandering in the desert for say, forty years or so, the Hebrews will have a renewed vigor in their role as chosen people."

Archangel Mazel Tov immediately stood up, breaking into enthusiastic applause. The vast majority of archangels followed suit, including Archangel Kvetch, who is famous for his brownnosing. It was downright embarrassing.

After the clapping died down, Beelzebub turned to face us. "Everyone here knows that the Hebrews were not your first choice as a chosen people. But it is evident that this congress is ready to give them a second chance. One hundred centuries ago, you were gracious to meet with Abraham to make the first covenant. Can we count on you to renew the covenant with Moses and release the Hebrews from their seven generations of Egyptian slavery? We trust you will negotiate a second covenant with whatever you feel necessary to ensure that the Hebrews will not fail again in their mission."

All eyes turned to us. We had to hand it to Beelzebub. He set us up like a bowling pin. How could we refuse to meet with this Moses character after such a show of sentiment? So after a motion by Archangel Mazel Tov to adjourn the congress and seconded by Kvetch, we held a private conference with Beelzebub. There we intended to learn more about Moses before meeting with him.

Beelzebub had some sage advice for me once we were sequestered from the others. "Remember, Moses was raised as a prince. Although he may be herding sheep now, he's no simple shepherd like Abraham. While he may have inherited the patriarch's persistent determination, he is quite sophisti-cated and not easily impressed. The Egyptian mysteries are no mystery to him. Best to appear to him in some form that is going to give him a sense of awe, grab his attention, and shake him up a bit. Maybe present yourself like a burning bush that talks but is not consumed."

We thanked Beelzebub and beamed ourselves down into that part of Midian where he told us we would find Moses tending his flock in the great valley south of the Dead Sea. There we found a good-sized thorny acacia bush on a little rise at the foot of Mount Sinai overlooking a green pasture that was perfect for grazing sheep. We ensconced ourself into the designated scrub and began to burn from within, careful not to consume it.

In the time it takes for spit to disappear on a hot griddle, a tall, distinguished human male herding a sizeable number of sheep made his appearance. The man we took to be Moses noticed us immediately and came closer. We spoke out to him in our deepest baritone voice, advising the man to approach no closer without taking off his sandals because he was entering holy ground.

To our surprise, he immediately removed his sandals and came as close as he dared without singeing his beard. We felt no fear emanating from him but rather a deep, intelligent curiosity. And much to our own satisfaction, we detected in him a bit of awe.

"Greetings my dear Moses. We appear to you in this particular form so you will not unduly lose your self-possession. Had you seen our countenance in all its glorious splendor, you would have soiled your tunic. Therefore, we have appeared to you as this lowly thorny acacia bush to commission you as chief emancipator, redeemer, and lawgiver who will lead your people out of Egyptian bondage."

"I assume you are the one true, unrivaled, universal god of Abraham, Isaac, and Jacob," he replied, a little too casually. We sensed that the bit of earlier detected awe was already dissipating.

"I was what I was, I am what I am, and I will be what I will be," we said mysteriously, hoping to compensate his flagging awe by piquing his still apparent curiosity.

Confusion flashed across Moses face for an instant before he regained his composure. "I'm not sure what that means but I do appreciate your appearing to me in your understated glory so that I might be spared the embarrassment of a soiled tunic. Never did I for one moment believe I would have the privilege of meeting the Source of Powers. What an honor! Your wanting to commission me in the roles you name to free my long-suffering people is very flattering. But as you see, I am but a poor shepherd not worthy of such privilege."

From the hint of condescension in his voice we could sense Moses was laying it on a bit thick.

"However, at the age of eighty, my current circumstance is an exciting enough existence. I am more than content with my simple shepherd's life. I've got a beautiful twenty-something wife, Zipporah, who thinks I'm the greatest thing since fried matzah. It's all I can do to keep her satisfied. The local physician has me drinking this concoction of horny goat weed mixed with several other foul tasting herbs to make sure my rod and my staff can still comfort Zipporah, if you get my meaning." With that, Moses winked knowingly.

We had to suppress a slight giggle. His ribald humor, verging on the vulgar, was not lost on us.

"When I first came to Midian, Zipporah's father, Jethro, hearing I was an exile from Egypt, gave me shelter, albeit in a very deep pit for ten years. Ten years! Can you imagine? Maybe it was some kind of test. Or maybe he was trying to kill me. Had not Zipporah dropped breadcrumbs down to me in that dank hole, I would have starved to death. I felt immense thankfulness to her, although I did develop a severe case of gluten intolerance.

"But after I passed Jethro's pit of starvation ordeal, he granted me Zipporah's hand in marriage, which I asked for in gratitude for her saving my life. And surprise, surprise, not only did Jethro grant my proposal, he also hired me to manage his already thriving shepherding business. As you can see from the size of this flock, one of many, by the way, Jethro's trust in my abilities was not in vain.

"And as if that weren't enough, even you, the supreme god of my fathers, can't imagine how excited and thrilled I am that Zipporah is with child, yet a second time. The soothsayer predicted this is to be the second of two sons. We named the first one Gershon, meaning "wandering stranger," which seemed appropriate for the son of a man in my situation. The one currently in the oven is to be named Eliezer in homage of the help I've received over the years from you, oh mighty Lord.

"No offense, but we're still undecided about circumcising them. As the all-knowing god of the universe, you're probably aware of how my mother, Jochebed, saved my life from Pharaoh's sword when I was an infant. There was no time for my own circumcision, and Zipporah is afraid that Gershon and Eliezer would develop a complex should they be circumcised with their father's schlong still intact."

We would have nodded thoughtfully had we not been in the form of a burning bush. "We understand your situation," we assured Moses, remembering how the circumcision clause was nearly a deal-breaker with Abraham. "We very much appreciate your naming your second son in honor of the help we have blessed you with during your entire life. Not every Hebrew is raised as a prince in the Pharaoh's palace."

We paused to give him a moment to contemplate that before continuing. "And we also appreciate the tragic circumstances surrounding your birth, which prevented your own circumcision. No one will accuse us of being a stickler god without compassion. At your age, how can we expect a remedial circumcision to comply? Other than killing those Egyptian taskmasters who were brutalizing your people, you have led a righteous life. Of course, you are also responsible for the deaths of thousands of the Pharaoh's enemies while leading his army into battle, but you were only taking orders.

"Your righteous life and certain of your other attributes are the reason we're commissioning you as the redeemer of the Hebrew slaves in Egypt. Therefore, we exempt you from the rite of circumcision. Of course, we do expect that your young son, Gershon, be circumcised, even though he is a year past the eighth day after his birth. And naturally, we expect that your as yet unborn Eliezer be circumcised as well, according to our original covenant made with Abraham."

A number of expressions passed across Moses' face as we talked, relief and alarm among them. We suspected that both were related to the subject of circumcision more than the prospects of being commissioned as the redeemer of the Hebrew slaves.

"I thank you for believing in my worthiness as the Hebrew redeemer. However, as I originally stated, I am content with my life as it now is. As I told you, things are pretty sweet for me right now. I'd be mad to return to Egypt, where I would face certain death for the murders I committed there. For me to enter the land of my birth would be committing suicide. At the same time, I am much relieved that you have exempted me from the rite of circumcision. However, as far as circumcising my sons, Gershon and Eliezer, as I mentioned, Zipporah has concerns. I could never agree to their circumcisions without her buy-in. Surely, you've heard the saying, 'Happy wife, happy life.'"

Our mission to recruit Moses as the great Hebrew redeemer was looking dicey. We needed to get him on board without Zipporah complicating the negotiations, so we had to sweeten the deal—fast.

"We can see there are some impediments in the way of accepting this great, noble, and necessary task. Therefore, let us assure your safety and success in returning to Egypt. Whenever you call upon us, the god of Abraham will be at your side assuring your protection. Not only will you be helping to free the Hebrews from bondage, you will be assisting in delivering the divine word of God to your people that will assure their righteous living. As far as circumcising your sons is concerned, your mission is much more important than some snippets of foreskin. Let Gershon's and Eliezer's members match those of their father."

Our big mistake was letting Moses see how eager we were to have him be the leader to free his people. He sensed our desperation and suggested we sweeten the deal even more. In addition to being ready to help him out of trouble whenever he invoked us, we also had to assure him that his name would be forever honored as the greatest leader ever known. We were asking him to take on a pretty big task, so we figured we could grant him this small boon to satisfy his ego.

But then Moses dropped the big demand. Since we were billing him as chief emancipator, redeemer, and lawgiver, he wanted us to promise he would have final editing rights over whatever divine words from us he was called upon to deliver to his people. Talk about chutzpah!

At the time, Moses claimed he needed editing rights because of his speech impediment. He did, in fact, have a bad stutter, so his request seemed reasonable given he would be doing a ton of public speaking. Foolishly, we agreed to his demand. How deeply we have come to regret that promise and how impactful it would prove to be on humanity's history!

5

Redeeming the Sinful Edits of Moses

FAST FORWARD NINE MONTHS TO just after Moses led the Hebrews out of bondage and onto the plains of Midian. Once these refugees established camp at the foot of Mount Sinai, where we first commissioned Moses, we asked him to climb higher up the mountain alone for what we believed would be a short editing conference—three to four days, max. To say that our patience was to be sorely tested would be an understatement.

We had already been in dialogue with Moses regarding the need for revising the original thousand-year-old covenant made with Abraham, both agreeing it was too vague and loosey-goosey, needing more specificity beyond the circumcision requirement. We also agreed that the opportune moment to present the Hebrews with the updated covenant would be ASAP after the exodus. That was the time they would likely be most receptive. But that was about the only thing upon which we agreed.

Archangel Gabriel, Heaven's primary wordsmith, had been busy drafting and redrafting "Humanity's Quick Setup Guide for the Three Divine Gifts of Intelligent Awareness" and *The Fifteen Statements*. We presented these to Moses at the start of our Mount Sinai meeting. The drafts were more than adequate, if a little wordy. Gabriel did have a habit of repeating himself, so we figured Moses would do some minor editing—maybe adding a comma here, breaking up a run-on sentence there. Boy were we in for a shock!

Saint Moses was not at all happy with that first draft, insisting that "Humanity's Quick Setup Guide for the Three Divine Gifts" be withheld entirely from the general population of Hebrews. We were outraged. We considered the guide essential for building capacity in humans to faithfully keep the suggestions outlined in *The Fifteen Statements*. Moses reminded us that we had promised him the final edits. What could we do? A promise is a promise.

When it came to *The Fifteen Statements*, Moses contended that after seven generations of slavery, a newly freed people would find them confusing. "The Hebrews have lost touch with exercising free will," he said. "They need hard and fast laws that give a sense of certainty. They need simple, straightforward commandments! Don't beat around the bush, burning or otherwise," he added, trying to interject a bit of levity, knowing he was stepping on some heavenly toes.

We were ready to compromise, but Moses brooked no compromise, insisting on calling them commandments, so our suggestions aimed at stabilizing an entire nation of newly freed slaves became commandments instead of suggestions.

Not only did Moses want laws instead of suggestions, he wanted them to be brief, and his version of brevity involved extremely heavy-handed editing. He whittled down a manuscript of length and depth to one that could be posted on a board like a menu.

We admit that our obsession with context leads us to provide more perspective that most humans can comprehend, and that has been an impediment. Omniscience has its limits. Our multifaceted, multidimensional view is all well and good, but we need to do a better job of crafting the message for the intended audience. That is why we felt compelled to call in Beelzebub on this project as coauthor.

"Humanity's Quick Setup Guide for the Three Divine Gifts of Intelligent Awareness" has not been available to the general public until now. Various iterations of it have been sequestered in certain mystery schools for thousands of years. Over the centuries, portions of the guide have found their way into a number of religious institutions—thoroughly mangling Heaven's original intent. It is now being made available to humanity here as a way of rectifying that problem, along with the full version of our ten suggestions before they were paraphrased by Saint Moses and called the Ten Commandments. As a nod to his contribution and to avoid confusion, we have left them as commandments. We are including five bonus suggestions—arbitrarily excluded, in our opinion, in the editing done by Moses, who had a fetish for the number ten.

That being said, Beelzebub did do a terrific job as wordsmith of our original drafts written more than two and a half millennia ago. He has managed to keep the general intent of those original counsels while making them more accessible for a modern audience. There were times when Beelzebub also added his own special brand of humor, which the average reader may find overly sarcastic. We, on the other hand, must own up to the bad puns, which were mostly inadvertent.

Even with our omniscience and omnipresence, we cannot predict what humanity will make of these writings, for we gave humanity the gift of free will at the point of creation. In other words, how humanity will take it is a crapshoot. But let us not end on a sour note. Looking back to our first draft, we are somewhat embarrassed to see how defensive we were feeling at the time. Perhaps we were still beating ourselves up for leaving humanity to pretty much fend for itself after the creation.

And please forgive us if you find some of these "commandments" somewhat overwrought. That tone was, no doubt, another reason Saint Moses did so much ruthless condensing. And after our injuries from parting the Red Sea, we were sympathetic toward Moses, who we feared might suffer the same fate trying to lift our earlier drafts.

That Saint Moses managed to whittle down our suggestions to fit on two tablets is something of a miracle. Looking back on it now, forbidding Moses the simple satisfaction of entering the promised land seems ungracious and overly harsh, especially after his forty years of of leading the Hebrews wandering through the desert.

Granting Moses the title "Saint" was a kind of consolation prize after denying him entry into Caanan. We simply snapped at his smashing our tablets after our five-week-long editorial haggling. Even though we understood his frustration over the golden calf incident, we had not even thought to make a copy of the tablets.

When Moses climbed back up Mount Sinai to ask us to chisel the whole thing again, we were still nursing a bad case of writer's cramp. Looking back on it, were we still harboring resentment over his editing job? You be the judge.

6

Humanity's Quick Setup Guide

BEFORE GIVING SAINT MOSES *THE Fifteen Statements* (eventually known to you as the Ten Commandments), we presented him with a draft version of "Humanity's Quick Setup Guide for the Three Divine Gifts of Intelligent Awareness." The consensus in Heaven was that the Hebrews would first need a working understanding of how to maintain the interdependent mechanics of the three divine gifts. Otherwise, they would not have the capacity to adhere to Heaven's counsels. How right that consensus proved to be!

Having just escaped multiple generations of toiling as beasts of burden, the Hebrews were totally clueless about who they were, where they were going, and what Heaven expected of them as our chosen people. We believed that just laying a bunch of seemingly arbitrary rules and regulations on a people who didn't know their pipics from their tushes would be a complete waste of the stone tablets on which the statements were carved.

But while Moses conceded that the information in the guide was essential, he still insisted that it stay hidden to all but an inner, esoteric circle of high priests within the Cohan and Levite tribes until the proper time. All of Heaven wonders if humankind would have had a better shot at avoiding its current critical conundrum had Saint Moses not been such an elitist snob.

The guide was designed for humanity to objectively see itself at all times and in all situations—a central capacity if one is climbing the evolutionary ladder. Objective seeing is a vital component for Homo sapiens if they are to keep Heaven's counsel beyond a couple of generations. Had it been broadly available, most every human would have mastered the basic elements and interdependent workings of its own psyche, which are essential for marshaling the clarity of awareness required for self-observation. Thanks to Moses, the fact that the guide has remained largely hidden has caused human objectivity to be as rare as a kosher shrimp wrapped in bacon, and humanity's evolutionary progress has long been at a standstill.

Considering the current planetwide consumer culture, has individual free will been diminished to the point that the vast majority of humans lack enough of it to develop the skill of reliable self-observation? The answer to that question remains outstanding—right along with whether yeti actually exist and if leavened bread is really all that bad at Passover.

Heaven admits that the unfortunate state of affairs requiring the guide was due to yet another oversight on its part. In creating the physical reality of Mother Earth, we were confounded by the tendency of matter to lose its attraction to itself. To make a long story short, to overcome physical matter's anticoagulatory properties, we created an invisible force we called uber glue. Known to you as gravity, we designed it to draw down all physical matter on Mother Earth toward her bosom.

Without such a force of attraction holding physical reality together, physicality tends to transubstantiate back into energy by way of the universe's innate pattern of continuous expansion. The whole point of creating a three-dimensional reality was to provide humanity with a physical incubator nurturing it to evolve beyond simple lifeforms. Heaven loves bacteria, viruses, and fungi, but those tiny, elemental creatures, sacred though they are, neither depend on gravity to reproduce nor have the capacity to become the cocreators we need.

Imagine Heaven's chagrin in discovering that gravity was working in parallel fashion on human consciousness. The law of uber glue, created to facilitate humanity's divine destiny, simultaneously became a major impediment to the expansion of human consciousness. How is that for irony? Turns out we made uber glue too sticky.

So instead of a cakewalk in the Garden of Eden as we had planned, almost all humans are saddled with having to make significant efforts to expand their own powers of awareness. And as you might have expected, this situation has proven to be a grave disappointment in Heaven. We had expected that well before now, humanity would have taken up shouldering some of the managerial burden of Mother Earth's delicate life-sustaining systems. We never imagined that humanity's arrested development would actively short-circuit those systems.

Not only had we not foreseen gravity's contracting effect on human consciousness, Heaven underestimated the uncurious, complacent, forgetful natures embodied by Homo sapiens. We were honestly shocked at how so few of you were willing to make the effort needed to become objectively aware of yourselves, nor had we imagined how the strength of denial would come to dominate your species.

Since so few of you notice that you are literally dreaming throughout most of your days, few strive to fully wake up. Most humans believe that when they open their eyes and get out of bed, they are no longer sleeping. Given that tragic yet understandable delusion, how could Heaven expect individual humans to make the required effort to awaken? Boy, do we have egg on our face.

To counterbalance gravity's contracting force on three-dimensional consciousness, we provided the three divine gifts of intelligent awareness, which can only be fully implemented when they're balanced together as a working whole. But because the guide remained hidden to all but the most determined among you, Humanity has, by and large, not been able to fully implement the three gifts. Instead, humans tend to become fixated on using one or at best two of them. Virtually no human ever attempts using all three of them to their full functionality—which means virtually all humans lead unbalanced lives between sleep and wakefulness without likelihood of fully awakening.

This version of the guide has been reworked to make it more user-friendly. We're sensitive to the pandemic disease of impatience infecting modern Homo sapiens, so we've made it a quick setup guide. A complete understanding of the information provided in the guide opens a portal to achieving the proper balance that will allow the three divine gifts to be fully used, which will thereby enable each individual to reach its divine destiny of cocreatorship.

Going through the portal offered in the guide requires a conscious decision, and gaining the balance required for the three divine gifts is achieved by taking up the work required once one has entered the portal. But be aware that gravity will automatically tug to keep you from staying inside the portal. Only your individual intention can overcome gravity's pull on your awareness.

Humanity's Quick Setup Guide for the Three Divine Gifts of Intelligent Awareness

Humanity has been endowed with three divine gifts: the physical body's intelligence, emotional intelligence, and intellectual intelligence. Here is a brief rundown of the three, presented one at a time.

Gift 1: Physical Body Intelligence

The physical body is the first divine gift because the other gifts would have no possibility of functioning without it. The body has several layers of intelligence and uses the language of sensation to communicate with the other two gifts of awareness.

In addition to its moving intelligence, the physical body has instinctual automatic sensing intelligence. Such intelligence allows the body to self regulate, which comes in very handy. Having to consciously take each breath or heartbeat would leave one with very little awareness left over for sensing moisture, dryness, weight, pleasure, or displeasure.

Through the senses of taste and smell, the body can determine which substance supplies sustenance and which is likely harmful. Without any conscious effort on your part, your body's instinctual intelligence knows how to absorb essential elements from food for its own regeneration while eliminating unessential elements. When injured, the body knows how to immediately begin healing itself.

Packaged within the physical body's instinctual intelligence are additional senses that apprehend and remember the patterned manifestations of light, form, and sound. By using the body's capacity to see, hear, touch, taste, and smell, these functions allow a high degree of engagement with the body's environment that would otherwise not be possible.

An even greater interaction with its physical environment is brought by the body's moving intelligence. Included in this intelligence is a sense that records spatial relationships and stores memory of learned movements. Though designed to learn and execute delicate motion, these learned behaviors can become habitual and coarse. To keep the moving intelligence from lapsing into gross mechanical movement, the body must continue to learn new movements throughout its existence.

The colors, shapes, and sounds registered by the body's instinctual intelligence can be imitated and purposefully arranged through the body's moving intelligence. Such purposeful arrangements, known generally as "art," act as representations that activates the second gift, emotional intelligence.

Gift 2: Emotional Intelligence

Emotional intelligence uses the language of feelings to communicate with the other two centers of intelligence. It too has multiple levels of intelligence like that of the body. The most basic of these intelligences is the least nuanced, most reactive part. Emotional sophistication on this layer is limited to like or dislike, attraction or repulsion. This is the lowest level, automatic functioning that responds to the obvious polarity comprising the physical environment.

At the higher layer of emotional intelligence is the capacity to lift the body's gross sensing perceptions of its immediate environment onto an etheric dimension beyond the apparent duality of physical existence. But this level of emotional intelligence is often overly influenced by an identification with "me/mine" and "other." To prevent such undue influence, attachment to any emotion is to be avoided.

Conscience functions in the higher level of emotional intelligence, bringing feelings of rightness and wrongness. The most evolved level of emotional insight comes with a recognition that one's life has purpose and emotes the desire to pursue that purpose. This higher layer is where an individual's personal will feels guided by divine intent, engaging the body's moving intelligence in the work of self-perfecting. This is also the level of emotional intelligence responsible for refining the proper functioning of the third gift, intellectual intelligence.

Without the refinement of divine intent available within the higher level of emotional intelligence, intellectual intelligence remains stuck in its lower, automatic functions, devoid of its true creative potential. Without its creative potential as derived from the connection to higher emotional intelligence, intellectual intelligence becomes dangerous.

Gift 3: Intellectual Intelligence

As you might have guessed, intellectual intelligence has caused the most controversy among the heavenly hosts. The gift of giving humanity the utility of words, concepts, reason, and logic was strongly opposed by many of our minions. To quote Archangel Bupkus, "Words can be assigned different meanings. Concepts can be twisted. Reason can become unreasonable and logic can become illogical. Even creativity can become destructive."

"Without proper guidance, thinking is prone to become delusional and even deranged," Archangel Mazel Tov added.

And it is true that along with the abilities of language, words, concepts, reason, and logic, the intellectual function invites a certain amount of imagination (most often fueled by the lower functions of the emotional and body intelligences) that ends up wasting precious attention through fetishizing trivia and physical cravings, detracting precious attention from humanity's ultimate mission.

As is apparent, most of our minions were willing to take that risk and voted to give humanity the gift of intellectual intelligence. They did this despite knowing that humanity might focus on a dualistic, absolutist perspective tending toward superficial conclusions and bad judgements.

The winning argument in favor of giving humanity intellectual intelligence was succinctly put by Archangel Nebbish. "The whole point of creating humanity in the first place was so it would take up its place helping to keep Mother Earth's delicate, reciprocal, interdependent systems in balance. Why would we withhold the essential function humanity needs to administer its management position?" Nebbish was always good at pointing out the obvious.

As with the first and second gifts, intellectual intelligence comes with its own set of higher and lower functions. And as with those previous gifts, Heaven intended that humanity fully utilize its highest levels. The controversy among our minions was whether most humans would be content to let gravity hold their intellectual intelligence down on the lower levels or whether they had the will to overcome gravity's hold.

Unfortunately for both Heaven and Mother Earth, those original fears plaguing a significant minority of our archangels were justified. With few exceptions, humanity has refused to step up to its destiny of cocreatorship. In fact, collectively, its overall behaviors have been antithetical to taking that step.

Each of the three gifts humanity has been given is composed of higher, more creative functions and lower, more mechanical, automatic functions. The lower, mechanical levels of functioning are not bad, in and of themselves. They're necessary for freeing the creativity found in the higher levels.

Mechanical thinking is quite useful. Without it, humanity would be lost within the physical dualistic maze of three-dimensional reality. When making your little daily plans, the use of automatic, lower level thinking can be most appropriate. The shortcoming of this mode is its rigidity and lack of relativity. When in control of intellectual intelligence, the mechanical function expresses itself through automatic reactions (often triggered by lower emotional intelligence) relying on preconceptions, arguments, and clichés.

Complicating the situation is that mechanical thinking stores memories haphazardly, leading to an associative, random thought process. Although associative thinking can be entertaining, especially to the person lost in its individual associations, associative thinking wanders, distracted and without purpose. It tends toward the nonsensical and its conjectures, sometimes posing as creativity, are often beside the point. Humanity's divine mission becomes eclipsed by the fascination of its own cleverness.

This mechanical, lowest part of Humanity's intellectual intelligence uses a simple absolutist form of cognition. Something, anything—a color, an odor, the weather, that person over there, a certain situation you happen to have an opinion about, this statement you just read or heard—is judged to be good or bad, right or wrong, or not applicable. No nuance, no analysis, no seeing the bigger picture is available on this mechanical level.

Even more problematic with this automatic operational mode is that it does not distinguish the difference between a previous, remembered experience and a new, never before encountered one. Such reactive thinking is primed for argumentation. Mechanical thinking's most often used, reflexive phrase is, "Yes, but." This level of thinking is *not* actual thinking.

The ultimate point of giving humanity the third gift, intellectual intelligence, was to endow humanity with the capacity to observe itself completely, objectively, analytically, without bias, and without preconceptions. Intellectual intelligence is that level where reason and logic keeps a check on runaway imagination. Its attention is held through will and effort, and there is nothing automatic or mechanical in higher order intellectual intelligence.

This higher order of thinking has the capacity to bring several possibilities to any given question. It also carries with it the ability to divide attention. It can see how and where one's body is functioning in the three-dimensional space while at the same time being aware of what emotions are present in the body and perceive the reasons such feelings are arising.

Intellectual intelligence invites the pondering of one's life in general and gives form and conceptualization to one's life purpose in particular. It does this through its ability to deduce the urgings of divine intent coming from higher emotional intelligence. Promptings from higher emotional intelligence are constantly being broadcast, but without the attitude of receptivity, intellectual intelligence tends to ignore them.

Maintaining an attitude of receptivity toward the promptings emanating from higher emotional intelligence is imperative for humans to engage intellectual intelligence optimally. Intuition, born outside humanity's three dimensions within physical time and space, is thus channeled to this aspect of the human, but it can only be grasped when the gift of intellectual intelligence is open, empty, and spacious. When it *is* open, it can translate the promptings of higher emotional thinking into possibilities and create divinely inspired abstract formulations. But for this divine alchemy to take place, intellectual intelligence must be trained to listen to higher emotional intelligence.

Without the proper training, humanity's ability to use its gift of intellectual intelligence at its highest capacity is thwarted, and it remains at the level of mechanical functioning. (Likewise, it must be said that without proper training, the same thing can be said for the first and second gifts: They will remain at a lower, mechanical level and not be fully actualized.) The potential of real creativity found in intellectual intelligence will not correctly interpret Heaven's urgings toward cocreatorship without this training in listening to higher emotional intelligence, and little will be accomplished other than the spooling of an endless tangle of conceptual confusion.

The capacity of observing oneself is contained within the higher levels of thinking achieved by developing intellectual intelligence. When seeing oneself objectively with impeccable, joyful attention, the mechanical, automatic operation in each of Heaven's three gifts assume their proper functioning. In this state of objective seeing, identification with the self as a separate entity recedes and humanity can move toward its cocreatorship destiny.

Humanity was created to live in alignment with the mission of cocreatorship. The personal will of each human fulfills individual destiny by being receptive to and acting upon divine guidance. In doing so, personal will renders service to all of humanity rather than to the narrow, often destructive goals dictated by identifying yourselves as separate from us.

We hope you find this guide helpful for humanity's proper use of its divine three gifts of physical body intelligence, emotional intelligence, and intellectual intelligence. Our original intention was that these gifts be used by humanity to take responsibility for its own further evolution. By analogy, if humanity is the "hardware" of Heaven, the three gifts are the necessary "software" making humanity fully functional cocreators.

Our bad for not including this guide with the original suggestions redacted by Moses as the Ten Commandments. Just remember, Moses believed the average human was not properly prepared to hear them. We apologize for any inconvenience or apocalypse this omission may have caused.

SCHWADRON
"TOO MUCH INFORMATION..."

7

First Commandment

The Moses Version: You shall have no other gods before us.

Heaven's Original Draft (Updated)
Children of Mother Earth's Humankind Project,

As your creator and source, our love for you is boundless and eternal. Since the inception of The Humankind Project on Mother Earth, our love for you is infinite, and we continue to provide for you unconditionally through our unending giving. You can never deny our generosity, for it will always be there to support you in all possible ways.

That being said, all we ask in return is a simple, constant, devotional faith in our sacred presence. By your active reflection of our unfailing love back to us, you lighten our burden. You strengthen our love throughout all of our creation. You become a sacred facilitator and cocreator. It doesn't get any better than that.

As you move more into alignment with our harmonious laws, your ultimate purpose as our cocreator here on Mother Earth is fulfilled. Having lived a life dedicating your daily thoughts, words, and deeds to our sacred remembrance, you will pass into eternity smiling, knowing that your family will continue to enjoy the style to which they have become accustomed.

Before ascending to your highest destiny as our cocreator, every human must, in his or her own way, seek to express unconditional love and care to all they encounter to the best of their ability. Acting thus, all adults affirm the loving welfare of themselves and those around them. In spite of what you may have learned, it is mutuality that really makes the world go 'round.

Unending blessings shower those who have their active faith in us and our harmonious, lawful ways to guide them. For as you've demonstrated on countless occasions, ignoring Heaven's divine guidance deprives you of your true humanity. To be born human is a rare and priceless gift not to be squandered by living as simple beasts, cute though they may be.

Although it may seem to you that there is a plethora of other gods worthy of your worship, these lesser gods are neither interested in your personal evolution nor that of humanity in general. Giving sacrifices to these so-called gods fashioned in stone, wood, earth, or metal keeps you bound to a life fixated on satisfying your fleeting physical desires and emotional whims. Devotion to the lower-tiered gods binds you to a repetitive, unfulfilling life filled with delusion, misery, and stagnation. Trust us, it's a bad trip.

Faith in our supreme divinity, an image that cannot be fashioned out of any three-dimensional material, demands you enter a divine realm beyond your limited sensory perceptions. You will never become fully human attending to only what you see, hear, taste, smell, or touch. These physical senses are the tools you have been given to help you build an invisible ladder toward higher perception. If you fail to fashion your own invisible ladder, blame not the tools.

Understand that when you place your faith in us and live your life guided by our laws, your entire life will be infused with higher consciousness that guides your thinking, behavior, and entire being. To know and understand Heaven's laws demands careful self-observation and an active, ongoing curiosity for studying our ways. Living up to your fullest potential demands that Heaven's invisible celestial energy guide your material animal natures. And just to be clear, although Heaven's celestial energy is invisible, it remains as obvious as the nose on your face.

Gods like Baal, Ishtar, Garuda, and Dagon may have many sincere followers, but these gods lack our redeeming qualities. We come before all other gods, named and unnamed. None of them have any of our superpowers. And no matter what rumors Abraham spread about us all those centuries ago when we made our first covenant with humanity, we do not expect the sacrifice of children as required by those pseudo-gods.

Just for the record, we did order Abraham to take his son up the mountain to the place of sacrifice. And yes, we did let Abraham think we expected him to kill Isaac. But let us be very clear about this: We would never have allowed Abraham to take his son's life. That is something you would expect from a Baal or a Garuda.

In testing Abraham's faith in us, we were conducting a critical demonstration. If one's faith cannot be shown as resilient and substantial, what have we but empty words? This is why Abraham and I settled on what was then Heaven's one and only consequential demonstration of sacrificial devotion: circumcision.

Since Abraham's time, things have become more complicated. After having been in slavery for the last seven or so of your generations, you have forgotten what it means to be our chosen people. Even keeping our circumcision agreement is now mindless habit. It's time to begin again. To fulfill your destiny while continuing to earn Heaven's protection, we want you to abide in all fifteen of these commandments. In this way, you will more surely raise your consciousness beyond your limited, tiring, ennui-inviting bodily lusts.

Having just been freed from your generations of bondage, now is an opportune time to renew your covenant with Heaven, assuming of course that you still wish to enjoy our protection by keeping your chosen people status. You're now officially on notice: Reinstate us as your God-in-Chief—your only God-of-gods—your Big Cheese God, way more powerful than Jupiter and Saturn put together.

Our supreme wish as your creator and the one, true, and only Source of Powers is that your abiding faith in us will result in your achieving higher consciousness and enacting that higher consciousness in your life. By doing so, may you then inspire hope for all humankind by lighting the way to Heaven's house. Our wish is that your joyful devotion to Heaven and our laws will bring into full realization your sublime latent capacities, thus allowing you to become our cocreator by virtue of returning our love to us and everyone around you—including your mother-in-law.

Living by Heaven's laws allows you a graceful, flowing resistance to the habitual slavery of your conditioned belief that you are separate selves. Living a harmonious, lawful life means supporting the highest purpose of each moment in which you find yourself. Unbounded blessings come to those who are humble, always striving to consider those around them. This is more than polite. It is evolutionary. And we are not just blowing smoke.

Accept with gratitude whatever honorable tasks you find before you that help awaken you from your self-centered natures. Actively choose whatever conscious labors are needed to be worthy of our chosen people. Surrender your obsessive thoughts of survival in order that you may be cocreators toward an upward evolutionary destiny. You were not born to simply consume another piece of bread, leavened or otherwise.

8

Second Commandment

The Moses Version: You shall make no idols.

Heaven's Original Draft (Updated)

Children of Mother Earth's Humankind Project,

Our love for you has freed you from lives of slavery in Egypt or any other land. We saw how you toiled those many years, mixing cement, cutting large pieces of stone, and lifting the cut stones one on top of another. In your extreme fatigue, we understand that you accepted the many graven images with which the Egyptians and others are so obsessed.

Sad to say, many of you forgot all about us, the one true Source of Powers. You began worshiping empty Egyptian statues with names like Osiris, Ra, and Horus. Such behavior is unbecoming of our chosen people, and now that you have been relieved from pyramid building detail, it is time to stop and come back to Papa. We will never ask you to fall on your knees and bow before any statues. In fact, we forbid you to build such things. By remembering us as your one and only

Source of Powers, you are free from bowing down to all those stone statues left behind from your bondage years. Our chosen people must never indulge in idolatry nor, for that matter, can you afford to be idle. (Our best puns are most always inadvertent. This was not one of our best.)

By a strong showing of faith in us, your existence is guided by a strong courage only bestowed by Heaven. If you want to continue carving those graven images you have become so fond of, that's on you. But don't expect help from Heaven when your precious little stone statue of Ishtar does bupkus for your failing liver after drinking all that Egyptian beer.

Soon, a time will come when you recognize that there is more to your life than what you can see, taste, touch, or hear. And the sooner you actively seek our invisible world where your true spirit dwells, the better it will be for you, your people, and Mother Earth. The time has arrived for transcending the unhealthy habits you took up as slaves and getting with Heaven's program.

As our freed and chosen people, you now have a big job ahead you. We understand that showing the rest of humanity how to live according to our salubrious yet invisible laws is no easy task. The external world is full of illusions, and many will continue to stay confused and in the dark. By constantly shining the light of our love burning within your own heart, you show the way for all.

No longer slaves, you have reached a new beginning. Continuing on as our chosen people demands more understanding than you have actualized thus far. You will need to up your game in the wisdom department. Our freeing you from slavery was influenced by sentimental nostalgia rather than any recent meritorious behavior on your part. Beelzebub made a gentlemen's bet with us that the Children of Israel would not last three full generations before they stopped obeying these new commandments. Be warned: We're sore losers.

What does upping your game look like? As mentioned, you picked up a lot of bad habits during your enslavement years. You still want to be our chosen people? It's now time to act like it, for God's sake! And we mean that literally. Stop with blaming the externals of your world. You want to blame somebody for your fate? Try blaming yourself for a change.

You have now been freed from slavery to whatever previous conditioning befell you. The shackles that hang on you and weigh you down are unlocked. You are free to drop them where you now sit. Arise and feel the power of your freedom. Just avoid getting too cocky. Once a people feel chosen and privileged, it's easy to grow an inflated sense of self. That's yet another reason for the original circumcision covenant with Abraham—less inflation.

It's only your continued thinking and behaving as if you are still slaves that keeps you from living as befits our chosen people. Become your own master and tame your beastly natures—which does not mean you cannot make a little whoopee when the mood strikes.

Though you are no longer working for the man, you cannot become a nation of slackers. Training your inner beasts to behave according to Heaven's laws will be an ongoing challenge. You are therefore advised to create support groups. Coming together at regular intervals with others battling the same demons is most beneficial. And a potluck after the meeting would not be bad either.

9

Third Commandment

The Moses Version: You shall not take the name of the Lord your God in vain.

Heaven's Original Draft (Updated)

Children of Mother Earth's Humankind Project,

While we expect your serious adoration and respect, as stipulated in the second commandment, we forbid you to kneel down to us. Okay, maybe we will allow it on Rosh Hashanah and Yom Kippur. We do this not out of humility but out of consideration for your arthritic elders.

You must love us with all your heart, all your might, and all your soul. You must love us so much that the whole world feels the depth of your sincerity. Whenever you invoke our name, make sure you do so for no other purpose than glorifying and praising us. The utterance of our name is reserved for those special times of worshipping us. To evoke a laugh with our name is an abomination. Nobody likes to be the butt of a joke, and we are no exception.

And while we touch on this subject, do not ever assert that we spoke to you directly. That would be dishonest and a total misrepresentation. It goes against our long-established policy of avoiding misinterpretation. And the total number of official messengers we have sent to you is less than the fingers on one hand, assuming we had a hand.

In the event you feel compelled to share some communication that you honestly believe we divinely inspired, proclaim you heard a mysterious voice in your head or a vision came to you in a dream. Tell them you heard it from the Oracle of Delphi or the I Ching. Just never say you heard it from us. Whenever you hear talking in your head, it is not our voice. That's not how we roll.

Your job is to inspire the glorious destiny awaiting all of humankind by becoming Heaven's cocreator. Never let the gentiles hear you referring to us in a less than respectful manner. Your whole gig as our chosen people will be cheapened by doing so. People sniff out insincerity. Paying lip service to your love of us is not enough. You have to really mean it, night and day, day and night. (We knew somebody would make a song lyric out of those words one day. And we were right. Gives you a whole new perspective on the song, doesn't it?)

We are not forbidding you to indulge in fun. A substantial celebratory element should be part of keeping Sabbath. A lot of you out there with a very good sense of humor. Loving you as we do, you will not be denied the pleasure of laughter—just not at our expense, if you get our meaning.

Since we see a lot of potential court jesters among you, we advise that your levity lean toward the self-deprecating variety. Making fun of yourself shows you are a vulnerable, approachable, and sympathetic person. You might also want to avoid sarcasm because too many people will take offense. But if you must resort to its use, limit it to politicians and lawyers. Otherwise it will come back to bite you in the tush.

Your task will proceed more smoothly by not letting the whole chosen people thing go to your head. Heathens are more likely to listen to you if they feel you're treating them as equals. You may be quick to recognize a good deal, but that doesn't mean you are any better than the barbarians. Stay humble.

Staying humble is easier if you stay in the truth. We do not speak of subjective truth influenced by your biased conditioning but rather the unadulterated truth. To recognize objective truth requires you to be present enough to perceive reality as it is. Your ability to be present to any moment expands with your keen awareness of what words issue from your mouth. Words uttered routinely contract your awareness. Our name is not a word ever to be spoken from habit.

Your brain is a most useful organ, to be mastered for increased awareness. Left to its own momentum, your brain, hypnotized by remembrances of past experience, tends to mistake its conditioned conclusions as objective truth. Impulsively acting on those conditioned assumptions will not further your mission. Clarity comes when your brain is dominated by the love of us in your heart and expressing it in your behavior—including your words about us, yourself, and my creation at large.

Teaching humanity about its responsibility for managing Mother Earth is a sobering task. The path is long and arduous. To avoid stumbling, make your serious yet joyous remembrance of our wisdom be the highest priority. Keeping Source of Powers on your side will make the effort much less daunting.

Just know that the beginning of the longest journey starts with the first step, and don't forget to pack an extra pair of sandals.

Due to the Law of Hazard, the Hebrews serve a pivotal position within our long-term plan for Mother Earth's Humankind Project. Inspiring humanity to become Heaven's cocreator is a heavy burden. Know that the avowed reverence for us by the descendants of Abraham, Isaac, and Jacob is central to the fulfillment of their mission. Just be careful not to become arrogant because of your chosen people status. It's so off-putting, not to mention alienating.

10

Fourth Commandment

The Moses Version: Keep the Sabbath holy.

Heaven's Original Draft (Updated)
Children of Mother Earth's Humankind Project,

Before your descent into slavery, your attention spans were much longer. As slaves for all those generations, your powers of concentration atrophied. Weak minds are not problematic for beasts of burden. But as our chosen people assigned to teach all humanity the gospel of cocreation, sustained concentration is indispensable.

You need to remember everywhere and at all times that your Source of Powers gives you the fruit of the earth, the rain from the sky, and all the good things you are free to enjoy. Your focused, heartfelt, loving attention to acknowledging our gifts is all we ask in return. Coming together in celebration and remembrance of our ways and laws will assure the success of your mission.

Understand that you are Heaven's personal representatives responsible for helping awaken all of humanity toward its upward evolutionary impulse. When you forget who you are and what is expected of you, our burden grows heavier. You lighten our load by remembering who you are and fulfilling your assigned mission as our cocreator and teacher of Best Mother Earth management practices.

To help you remember your sacred mission as our chosen people, set aside one day a week as a holy Sabbath in remembrance of us and our commandments. Make our holy Sabbath a solid sundown to sundown period in which you do nothing but celebrate us and rest. During that period, refrain from occupying yourselves with anything related to work. Eat, drink, and be merry. Consider it a party with prayer. You can sing a little, dance a little, and even make romance a little.

But in between all the celebrating and whoopee making, don't forget the praying. Include some serious discussion of what we expect from you as responsible, mature humans. Make this a regular practice without fail, starting at the end of every workweek. Once you get into this weekly rhythm, you will not only find it easy, you will find that setting aside this day for us will allow you to focus on your regular work the other six days of the week. Chosen or not, people still have to make a living.

Never let observing the holy Sabbath become a charade. If you go through the motions without sincere feeling, you need not bother. As much as we wish you to prosper, multiply, and teach the cocreation wisdom to the greater humanity, your success depends on your consistency and dedication.

You should also know that after a hard workweek, having a Sabbath is the pause that refreshes. Consider the value of rest to your precious gift of physical wellbeing. We did not design the human body to be abused. It is a regenerative miracle. With proper care, these parts will last seventy or eighty years without wearing out.

Since you're acting as our agent, it would be good that on the Sabbath you make a high impression. Put on some nice clean clothes and eat an extra-tasty meal or two. And it would make the time more distinctive if you kept a separate set of dishes used only for the holy Sabbath.

Keeping a weekly holy Sabbath is not only the most enjoyable practice to remember who you are and what is expected of you, it's also the easiest way to do it. Keeping the holy Sabbath means that for every seven days of your life, one of those days is devoted to sacred celebratory remembrance of Heaven and its concerns. Keeping the Sabbath holy means putting aside your day-to-day strivings and endeavors so every seventh day of your life is a renewal of your covenant with us, your one-stop Source of Powers.

Observing our holy Sabbath helps you to remember those ways of being you once manifested before slavery. By refamiliarizing yourself with our directives, you retrain yourself in the ways proper to a chosen people. Each holy Sabbath you keep drives the sense and aim of your existence deeper into your being-presence. And if you haven't figured it out by now, the aim of your existence is about leaving the planet better than you found it.

Aside from the nostalgia aspect of being our original chosen people back in Abraham's day, we confess that in bringing you out of the land of Egypt, we had our own personal agenda for giving you a second chance. Please accept that, in return for reinstating your freedom, we expect you to live up to your proper destiny as chosen people for all the reasons discussed above. You should also know that we have a bet with Beelzebub on whether you will live up to that destiny. He's betting you're not going to fulfill your mission for setting an example on how to treat the planet respectfully. Prove him wrong.

Keeping at least 24 out of every 168 hours set aside in rededication to us helps assure Heaven's blessings upon you. Never fear that you will not be given the means to prosper and multiply. Simply reduce the materialism, work less, rest, and take the day to appreciate these gifts. And in all that prospering and multiplying and observing and teaching and behaving properly as chosen people, you fulfill our wish of helping to fuel the fires of creation. And that's crucial because lately, we're feeling a bit like one of those statues of Atlas holding up the world. The stress is getting to us.

11

Fifth Commandment

The Moses Version: Honor your father and mother.

Heaven's Original Draft (Updated)
Children of Mother Earth's Humankind Project,

As implied in the previous commandment, your diminished attention span is of great concern to all of us. Moses had hardly ascended Mount Sinai to meet with us when your artists began forging a golden calf for you to worship. A bull, symbol of power, we could understand. But a calf?

We despair about the way you treat your elders. Their wisdom guided sustainable practices, treating the planet with respect, until the last couple of centuries. Now instead of being revered for their wisdom, they are poorly treated in assisted living. This is no way to transfer the knowledge. Have some respect.

What is even more unsettling is the percentage of you unable to remember what you ate for breakfast—especially disturbing because the only sustenance you've eaten since escaping Egypt is the manna Heaven rains down on you every morning. Have some respect for Heaven too.

And while we're on the subject of manna, it took a lot of chutzpah to complain about the dryness of Heaven's bread given without any cost to you whatsoever during the escape from Egypt. First of all, it was gluten free, which was part of the reason it was on the dry side. Second, we wanted manna to which the desert sand would not stick. Gritty is way worse than dry. A few years in the desert noshing on sand-covered manna and your teeth would have been ground to nubs. And third, it was whole grain manna, which meant it had plenty of fiber in there to keep you regular.

Bad as your short-term memory is, it is your long-term memory that has us really nervous. Being chosen people is one helluva task, and you cannot afford the energy to reinvent the wheel every day, if you get our meaning. You have to keep better records of all the collected wisdom once catalogued through the conscious labors of your ancestors. We know you were in a big hurry to get out of Egypt, but what a shame you lost all those ancient scrolls. Gathered over many generations, there was a passel of essential data recorded on them that would have helped you fulfill your destiny. But—hint—check out the caves. Lots of scroll stuff gets discovered in those dark, hidden places. Just ask Beelzebub.

Those who preceded you recognized the need to study and know our life-affirming laws. By objectively learning the reciprocal nature governing the universe, your foremothers and forefathers gained the strength of courage to place their faith in us. They knew down to their kishkes that Heaven's unwavering support of them comes from aligning with its harmonious laws.

Your freedom from slavery is not a license to forget the hard-won lessons of previous generations. Your ancestors did not sweat and toil to discover those laws of universal mutuality so their children could waste that precious understanding by indulging in their own personal pleasures, reactive emotions, and uninformed imaginings. Be faithful to your forebears as they were to us. Never forget the lessons they handed down to you and never forget that even the most senile among you has a bit of objective wisdom to impart. Elders are worthy of your love, kindness, and respect. An occasional visit around the holidays would be nice.

So important is retaining the objective knowledge once known to your ancestors that you need to honor them in special ceremony. Perhaps light a few candles on the anniversary of their death. That's always a good thing. You could say a special prayer in remembrance of their eternal souls. It would be really nice if on those occasions you tell your children stories about the more memorable things your parents said or did.

The *how* of honoring your ancestors is not as important as the *why*. Feel free to make up your own rituals for honoring them. We are not as concerned with the specifics as with those mentioned in keeping the Sabbath. The gist here is that you find a way to honor your ancestors, recall all the good things they did, and never forget that if not for your father and mother, your soul-stuff would have never congealed into your present incarnation.

If you start with your immediate family, like your own mother and father, you can use some of their traditions for how they honored their parents. The important thing is remembering who they were and the right actions they took that made your world a better place. Maybe it was that time when your mom kept you home from school because you had a sore throat. Or maybe your father offered to talk to that abusive taskmaster of a football coach on your behalf.

You don't need to stress out. This is just about remembering what should never be forgotten. And from what we have seen, you all could use an upgrade in the memory department.

You stand on the shoulders of those who came before you. Nobody arrived in this life without the help of countless others. The selfless deeds and achievements of your ancestors you now benefit from are the gifts you must add on to and pass to your children, should you be so blessed.

No one is an island unto themselves. You are all more like a whole bunch of little peninsulas sticking out from one big continent of humanity. Think of yourself as one little hair growing out of Mother Earth's body. The only difference between you is that some of you are growing out all silky smooth while others are all kinky and curly. Of course, kinky and curly is also part of your heritage. None of you would be here if not for those who came before you. Remember them and be grateful.

12

Sixth Commandment

The Moses Version: You shall not murder.

Heaven's Original Draft (Updated)
Children of Mother Earth's Humankind Project,

There is nothing on Mother Earth more special and more sacred than a human life. Our one exception is the life of Mother Earth herself, the holy sustainer of all life. Your technology and your teeming populations could threaten to overwhelm Mother Earth's vitality and her delicate ecological systems, which Heaven's team took such care in balancing—although, not to brag, it only took us a day. We're not so much worried about Mother Earth's life as the lives of the billions of your kind.

This is not to say that the fish swimming in the waters, the birds flying in the skies, or the worms burrowing in the soils are not sacred to us. These creatures are just as sacred as human life. But only humans have cocreation potential. This commandment is not about political correctness or whether the consideration of hierarchies is ever appropriate. Just use your common sense when it comes to prioritizing. That is what lists are for.

We're not expecting you to live on fruits and vegetables alone. A little animal protein may be necessary every once in a while, especially if you have concerns about the fragility of your bones. And for those among you with cholesterol issues, you may want to go easy with cheese, butter, milk, and eggs. It may be that your optimum health requires a bit of chicken, fish, or lamb flesh. This we can live with. But there are some creatures (see Deuteronomy 14:8) we prefer you not consume.

Suffice it to say that human life, in particular, must never be taken by another human for any reason whatsoever, even in retribution for the taking of another human's life. Which, by the way, is hardly ever the reason you murder each other anyway. Most of the time you're killing each other while in the grip of some unbecoming emotion such as jealousy, rage, or coveting either your neighbor's oxen or his wife's tush. Some people are even killed over disagreements based in abstract concepts. That is just so unacceptable. As our chosen people, we expect better. And Tribe of Bibi, please pay special attention.

Unfortunately, many of you did not survive the flight out of Egypt, and as you know, not a few of you even chose to stay there to continue living as slaves. Stockholm syndrome? Call it what you will. We did our part. Your entire population is but a tiny minority of humans on the planet, and given the critical importance of your mission, we need every man, woman, and child among you. This is an all hands on deck time in which we cannot afford to lose anyone. BTW, We're sorry we didn't warn you against moving to Germany sometime back. We should also have warned against moving to Austria and Poland. Those omissions on our part contributed to the numbers thing, but hey, you did a fine job of managing through it.

There is no need to become paranoid about your minority status. As long as you keep our commitments outlined in this document, Heaven will protect you from the often biased, brutish, war-driven behavior to help you thrive. Killing brings on the karma to be killed.

When you find yourself in any circumstances that contain a need to defend your behavior, violence becomes inevitable, and before you know it, somebody gets killed. If you want to prevent unnecessary enmity from those ignorant of our laws, consider professions in education or the study of physical laws. You're less likely to attract anger if you perform a useful service teaching the young or expanding on string theory.

But to be on the safe side, avoid professions that involve money lending, tax collecting, or lawyering. The goyim will come to resent you even if you give reasonable interest on their loans. And even if the king for whom you are collecting taxes is a righteous ruler, his subjects will still get jealous. When someone is feeling anxious and helpless, it's only natural to lash out at the middle man.

Desperate people make no distinction between their real oppressor and those acting as the oppressor's agent. Even if you do a certain amount of pro bono work for clients, lawyer jokes can get vicious. We also advise abstaining from becoming a landlord. Land speculation, while certainly profitable, can quickly become an exploitive pursuit. Evicting some poor widow and her six kids onto the street is not going to win you any friends.

And while it may seem convenient to take up dealing in precious metals or gemstones against the possibility that some intolerant king orders you to pack your bags and leave his country immediately, it can be a dicey way to make a living. Not that you are forbidden to do so, but bear in mind that engaging in such dealings invites a certain amount of danger. In truth, keeping precious items on your person is tempting someone to break both the eighth and tenth commandments. Don't say you weren't warned.

You were not brought out of the land of Egypt to profit by carrying out the dirty business of the ruling class. How is this different from the slavery from which you were freed? We are not telling you not to make a living. Just be sure that your business dealings are kosher and on the up and up. You will make fewer enemies and avoid being expelled from whatever country you happen to be living in. You will also not have to walk around with a knife under your tunic.

If we had wanted some ruthless tough guys as chosen people, we would have made a covenant with the Assyrians, who have no compunction about killing. In some ways, they would have been a better choice. When you're a superpower, there is an automatic fear/respect factor at play, and a lot of people automatically fall in line. That being said, what the world needs now is love, sweet love. We said it first.

13

Seventh Commandment

The Moses Version: You shall not commit adultery.

Heaven's Original Draft (Updated)
Children of Mother Earth's Humankind Project,

As mentioned in the previous commandment, human life is most sacred to Heaven because only humans have the potential to consciously contribute to creation by returning our unending love. Whenever we receive your love and devotion, the circuit of creation is completed, encouraging us to continue in our job as the one true source of all that is. Sad to say, for too long, not enough of humanity has actively returned our love, leaving us feeling somewhat discouraged. At times, we have even toyed with the idea of early retirement.

From the beginning and ever onward, we have freely subsidized Mother Earth with our creative energy, hoping against hope that at some point, her growing humanity would start paying off her accruing creative energy debt. What with all the other promising planets in this region of the galaxy potentially harboring organic life and needing more of our attention, we would be foolish to continue funding that debt for eternity. Our pockets may be deep, but everything has its limits.

Therefore, we hereby commit our creative energy to Mother Earth for another century or so on condition that humanity begin implementing sufficient measures to reduce the debt. Waking up the pagans and barbarians to the reality that human-kind has a debt to the forces sustaining it is your bottom-line mission. You should also let the rest of humanity know that the interest on its debt is reasonable.

To accomplish your mission, my chosen people need to make up for all that lost time spent being slaves. You need to get serious at organizing a more self-sufficient humanity willing and able to return our love in full measure and to do so as quickly as possible. You would not have been chosen if we thought you were not up to the task.

In some ways, you might consider your time spent as slaves as a blessing in disguise. If nothing else, the Egyptians were pretty fair at city planning, although they could have imple-mented sidewalks. During your long years there, many of you picked up strong organizational skills that can now aid you in accomplishing your mission. Chosen people need to have courage, strength, and the know-how to plan. To paraphrase a brilliant quote (which we inspired), never doubt that a small group of SOP-loving chosen people can change the world. It just may take a lot longer than one might have imagined.

Humanity was created for Heaven's purpose of closing the creative energy deficit gap Mother Earth has been running since her creation. The Hebrews probably know better than most that running a business in the red cannot go on forever. Fortunately for all concerned, once organic life began breeding on Mother

Earth, Heaven's natural laws of release, recapture, reabsorb, and recycle (AKA Heaven's composting plan) kicked in and began shrinking the huge creative energy deficit that Mother Earth had accumulated. That meant we did not have to work as hard as we did in the beginning. That was the good news.

The bad news is that our vast powers continue to fade over time. We're losing our focus more and more often and not feeling as driven as even ten millennia ago. Heaven's minions have suggested we start seeding younger, more attractive planets. To make matters worse for Homo sapiens' fate, the amount of creative energy we are able to recapture through the passive death of the organic life process seldom keeps pace with our ongoing diminution.

On occasion, one of your senseless wars destroys enough of your kind to relieve Mother Earth of some of her energy deficit for a short time. And those deaths resulting from earthquakes, typhoons, plagues, droughts, fires, and other natural disasters also return a bit of our precious creative energy. But Heaven can no longer count on those random peaks of passive organic death on an ongoing basis. Besides, surplus comes with its own problems. What Heaven really needs is for humanity to figure out how to better manage Mother Earth's inherent systems designed to produce a balanced, even, sustainable flow of energy.

As efficient as Heaven's composting plan is at helping replenish its creative energy back to Source, a significant amount is lost during the transmission process to Mother Earth. In the long run, whatever creative energy that can be recycled from the passive death of organic life back to us will not stop our own creative resources from diminishing. Even limitlessness has limits. If we are to continue in our role as Source of Powers for what already seems like an eternity, humanity must, sooner than later, grab its destiny by the *beitzim*. Remember, fellows, you may have a tiny bit less of that part above, but your *beitzim* are very much intact.

The former Hebrew slaves are to teach all of humanity its responsibility to become fully human. Chosen people must show humanity how to activate its creative powers, which are now overshadowed by its animal nature. Teach humanity to rise above being a mere prisoner of creation by becoming cocreators. Start acting like chosen people and establish a strong, reliable circuit of creative energy between humanity and Source.

If my chosen people are going to build a working grid of creative energy flowing back to Heaven, you must increase the current numbers of individuals prepared to generate the necessary force. The most efficient way to make that happen is for you to grow your now meager population as quickly as possible by organizing yourselves around a basic family unit. Each such unit must act as a strong container inside of which succeeding generations are well prepared to continue the mission with which you are now charged.

Our intention here is that each family unit be committed to a serious pace of rapid breeding. To ensure efficiency, each adult within the basic family unit must commit to marriage vows of fidelity to each other, thereby forging a hardened, leakproof container between them. Protecting the container of the family unit requires that all responsible adults within it devote themselves in all ways to each other.

The first thirteen years of each child's life shall serve as adequate preparation for a full understanding of responsible adulthood and participation in Heaven's mission. Nearly two full cycles of the seven-year itch will have culminated after the last child bred within the marriage has reached its responsible age. At that point, it may be that the breeding adults within such a marriage will either rededicate themselves to each other or, if all goes amok, seek renewal with an alternate marriage. But don't forget that in the Hebrew matrilineal culture, wives generally get to keep the tent. Just saying.

As of now, the Children of Israel are not producing enough well prepared children to continue its mission of teaching all of humanity how to reliably generate enough creative energy to keep Mother Earth's systems in balance. Therefore, we urge that you go forth and set up the holy institution of marriage to breed enough of your kind to fulfill your destiny as chosen people.

Now, in hindsight, Heaven grossly miscalculated how billions of people would exceed Mother Earth's carrying capacity. When we said, "Go forth and multiply," we didn't mean exponentially.

14

Eighth Commandment

The Moses Version: You shall not steal.

Heaven's Original Draft (Updated)

Children of Mother Earth's Hudmankind Project,

You have been given a difficult task that will take tremendous cooperation among your entire population. Having observed you for a couple of millennia, Heaven knows how snippy certain members of your various tribes can become should they feel slighted by another. Such smallness seems to run rampant among you and will severely impact your nation's ability to act in our name. Your grasping, greedy, jealous natures are tiresome, and the time to get over it is now.

Beelzebub, always ready to play devil's advocate, is quick to point out that there are dozens of Aunt Idas among you refusing to speak to their nephews because those nephews never sent bar mitzvah thank-you notes for the gifts selected and sent with such care. These commandments are designed to override any kind of pettiness that will foil your mission. So to all the Aunt Idas out there—enough is enough with getting your undergarments in a knot.

You need to rise above any personal feelings that block genuine love and compassion for each other. We wish to see more forgiveness and gratitude for each other because all those emotions generated by your overbearing, unrelenting self-obsession are not becoming to chosen people. The pagan barbarians need to see your nation as righteous, accepting, and generous. No one will listen to a bunch of lying, cheating thieves always on the lookout to take advantage of each other.

As outlined in the previous commandment, the basic family unit of responsible adults breeding and preparing their children for responsible adulthood is foundational for building a nation representing itself as Heaven's chosen people. However, while each family unit is a basic building stone, the love and compassion given within the family must extend to all other family units as well. You will not succeed in your mission if you're stingy with the resources you have managed to gather within your family unit.

Cultivate generosity, even toward those to whom you may not be directly related. Generosity is its own reward. Do not be afraid to give until it hurts. If you want to feel safe in your own home, you would do well to avoid piling up stores because doing so invites jealousy and thievery. How many sheep and goats does one family need before feeling they have enough? And BTW, avoid raising pigs. Kashrut aside, their short legs will never accommodate your nomadic lifestyle.

In getting caught up with you and your family's survival, you will miss the big picture. Pulling off your divine mission requires major cooperation among your entire population. Given your small numbers, if your mission is to succeed, you must eliminate intrafamilial squabbling—for any reason, even with your brother-in-law.

Gratitude is the attitude that will be most helpful in preventing the urge to steal. Gratitude will get you through this current awkward transition in which you find yourself. You must at all times realize that what your neighbors have, they deserve, and what you have is enough. In addition, keep a little loving kindness and forgiveness in your thoughts for your neighbors. You're going to need it.

We understand that to you, envy and greed are as natural as breathing. We say to you, see how such lowly feelings limit you in your capacities. You must put aside the majority of your survival-driven sentiments by cultivating a constant remembrance of your sacred mission. Not only are you your brother's keeper, you are also your sister's, mother's, father's and even Aunt Ida's keeper.

Before you signed onto your mission, Moses made it clear to you that Heaven expected a willingness to do whatever it takes. You will not accomplish the job without reconciling yourself to being as generous, kind, and forgiving to those outside your immediate family as to those within it. Israel will have to build a powerful unified force field built on a common fidelity overarching your twelve tribes or however many of them are left. And that includes all members of the tribes of Dan and Levi, who, we have noticed, often come off as a bit too self-important. And the Bibi Tribe—don't get us started.

While we're on the subject of tribes, you must humbly entreat and embrace your cousins who have dwelt in the land of Canaan longer than your captivity. These are your relatives who stayed in Canaan, not going down to Egypt with you. Pray those cousins accept you back to the homeland.

If your two peoples are to come together to forge a new, mighty nation entrusted with our sacred mission, be advised to share your good fortunes with each other. Never allow jealousy and covetousness to affect your relationships. Never hesitate to err on the side of generosity. Make it a win-win for everyone.

And of course, the same holds for others who still live in that land and also consider it their home.

Not stealing is good karma. When you leave home, what a godsend it will be to not even have to lock your door. What neighbor in their right mind would ever think of stealing from you when they're not feeling greedy or envious? Our advice: Not showing off is the best way to avoid inciting greed or envy in your neighbors. Showing off is not a good look.

15
Ninth Commandment

The Moses version: You shall not bear false witness against your neighbor.

Heaven's Original Draft (Updated)

Children of Mother Earth's Humankind Project,

Besides stinginess, greed, and envy, what really chaps our tuchus is lying. And while we're at it, gossiping is another big no-no. In fact, if time and space permitted, "Thou shall not gossip" would be its own commandment. Nothing erodes trust within a community faster than telling lies and unflattering stories about one another.

Who are you going to trust if those around you are lying and telling stories about you? Lying is never a good thing. Stay truthful. Be honest, even if your wife should ask if her toga makes her look fat. Of course, you may want to reframe her question before you blurt out something stupid you may later regret.

Honesty is the best policy when it comes to creating strong community, and refusing to lie to yourself makes it less likely you will lie to others. Of course, that's easier said than done. Not lying to yourself means you have enough objective awareness to see your true motivations in your thoughts, words, and deeds. Talk about a challenge! While many of you may have the courage to at least attempt an objective self-honesty, few of you have the strength of enduring focus needed to observe yourself at all times without bias. Remember, nowhere have we said that being chosen people was going to be all roses. If you're truly devoted to both us and our mission, you will need sincerity of faith underlying all you do.

This does not mean you should not laugh. Laughter can be a healthy response to life's little absurdities. We like a good laugh as well as anyone. But do not allow cynicism to creep into your humor. A cynical people may breed many comedians but will never accomplish our mission. As of yet, there are no statues dedicated to cynics—which is not to say there never will be. Even we can't know how degenerate your race might become.

This commandment assumes that you see the need for honesty and sincerity in accomplishing your mission. Honesty leads to trust. Trust leads to faith, and we guarantee there will be times when you will be needing a mountain of faith.

Although recognizing honesty's importance is a beginning, merely seeing the challenge without making genuine efforts will not get you where we need you to go. Accomplishing the mission means engaging with your understanding so it transforms into action. Every time you see yourself being dishonest, whether with yourself, your family, or your neighbors, the very recognition of it requires that you change your behavior.

At the risk of repeating ourselves, lying to yourself means you will lie to your neighbor, and trust will vanish. And how in our name do you think you will complete your mission without total cooperation among you? To be an example of what it is to be fully human requires an unprecedented cooperation and trust between all members of all your tribes. You will never obtain such cooperation and trust unless you agree to tell the whole truth and nothing but the truth, starting with yourself.

16

Tenth Commandment

The Moses version: You shall not covet.

Heaven's Original Draft (Updated)
Children of Mother Earth's Humankind Project,

This, our tenth commandment, may seem redundant, especially to those of the Cohan and Levite Tribes who think they know it all. Certain elements of this commandment do, in fact, allude to the eighth commandment with regard to theft of another's property. But this commandment is a deeper dive.

Besides the obvious no-no of taking that which is not freely given to you, when it comes to thievery or any such behaviors unbecoming to chosen people, simply refraining from those overt behaviors is not enough. Without the awareness of your inner attitudes and hidden motivations, you will continue to suffer in spite of your outward actions.

As you have probably noticed, our commandments are a collection of "do nots" with a few "dos" sprinkled in. This commandment in particular deals with the underlying agendas of unbecoming behaviors. This is not to absolve you from carrying out your worldly duties. Should your actions fail to adhere to the demands of these commandments, consider our covenant with you null and void.

Do not assume that this commandment is of lesser importance because it was the last one Moses allowed to be given to you. It is of no less importance than our first commandment, and in fact, we could have easily reversed them because they both deal with inner attitudes, fears, and desires. In other words, both the first and tenth commandments are the invisible sources from which outward behaviors arise.

Here's the deal: Before your enslavement, you had an inner practice that guided your outward behaviors. But jealousy arose among you and your relatives sold you into slavery. During your time in captivity, you managed to hold on to some of the outward trappings of a righteous people, but you lost the inner practice that once guided you.

Consider this commandment a reinstatement of the inner practice that imbues your outward actions with bedrock sincerity. Without this inner practice, you are mere empty togas blowing in the wind. Let these actions be founded upon the convictions of your heart. And you're way out of practice with that.

Our minions do not have the time to monitor every one of your innermost thoughts. What a nightmare that would be! You're your own best monitor. In all and in everything, learn to observe yourself. By creating an internal, objective self that joyfully watches your thoughts and feelings, you become aware of those motivations either strengthening your mission or subverting it.

But unbiased self-observation is a learned skill that reveals whatever fearful motivations are hindering your capacity for self-honesty. Freedom from your conditioned, egotistical thoughts, learned since birth, is the only true freedom.

Once you see the ruthless, one-track nature of your conditioned self, you will see the value of your constant observation of it. It's critical, though, to avoid self-flagellating when you catch yourself in these conditioned thoughts. Simply see how they are birthed from your innermost fears, which have been handed down to you, and send them on their way.

In all things, remember that you solemnly volunteered to be our chosen people. You accepted being impeccable examples for the rest of humanity. Teaching humanity what it means to be fully human is the whole point of our needing a chosen people. By your example, those ignoring these commandments may come to learn that there is more to human existence than living in the prison of their own animal natures.

In seeing the blessings from on high that a people who are fully human enjoy, the rest of humanity will learn by your example. They too will want to be fully human. They too will learn that living as our cocreators, leaving Mother Earth better than they found it, is better than an orgy and has none of an orgy's STD risks. At least, that's our plan.

This is not a time for half measures. Humanity is in a mess right now, and you should know that some of Heaven's minions have suggested flooding the world yet again and starting over. But we're not going to let our baser instincts prevail—for the moment. We'll keep our end of the bargain, continuing to guide and bless you, provided you continue adhering to these commandments with sacred, devotional feeling.

These ten commandments are interdependent, each reinforcing the others in subtle and not so subtle ways. They are not just simple rules to live by. They do hold you to an outward conduct in ways proper to representatives of a higher calling. But more importantly, when conducted with wholehearted love and sanctity, these commandants raise your inner vibration, and by extension, raise the vibration of Mother Earth.

Your ultimate mission is to show all of humanity that generosity of spirit and putting the other before oneself leads to a life of the fullest satisfaction. By your example of living without coveting, unending blessings will be showered down upon you. Being grateful for what you have is its own reward. Do that and this whole gig will work out for all involved.

Time is quickly running out to get the majority of humanity on an upward evolutionary trajectory. As an added incentive, to help prevent you from flagging in your mission, we're putting a little of the fear of God in you. If the bulk of humanity does not start shaping up and showing up for its higher destiny of cocreatorship, it will not be the water but the fire next time.

NEW RELEASES
11.
12. THOU SHALT
13. THOU SHALT
14. THOU SHALT
15. THOU SHALT
16. THOU SHALT
17. THOU SHALT
18.
19.
20.
SIZEMORE
CartoonStock.com

17
Eleventh Commandment

Summary of Eleventh Commandment, Omitted by Moses: Thou shall not be greedy.

Children of Mother Earth's Humankind Project,

Greediness is a true affliction that undermines humanity's cocreative potential. And BTW, there is no Saint Moses version of this commandment. As previously stated, Moses asserted that ten commandments were a good round number for marketing purposes and more than enough for a population of confused, newly freed slaves. And since we had foolishly allowed him editorial license, he made full use of it, deleting this and four other essential commandments.

Besides limiting our commandments to just ten, Moses also insisted that forbidding greed had already been addressed in the tenth commandment. Knowing Moses as we do, had he agreed that greediness deserved its own commandment forbidding it, he would have whittled it down in his typically terse style to something like, "Thou shall not be greedy."

Saint Moses was not the most nuanced of prophets. Having a severe hipper than thou complex, Moses was quite convinced of his own infallibility. Still, he had invaluable talents needed for the exodus. Sometimes the bad must be overlooked for the sake of the good. Just ask Beelzebub.

To be clear, the tenth commandment addresses an individual's inner suffering when tormented by the gnawing feeling that they are not enough. Entertaining that lowly emotion invites your own personal heartache, resentment, envy, and tsuris. Greediness takes coveting to a whole other level, further undermining humanity's cocreative potential. Greed manifests outwardly by gluttonous, selfish, devouring behavior, always grasping for more and more. Whereas while under the spell of coveting, you simply eat yourself up with envy from your head down to your kishkes. Coveting can be considered the gateway emotion leading to the hoarding habit.

While not expressly forbidden in the previous commandments, hoarding can lead to adultery and/or stealing. And even if you can limit your hoarding to just pillows, animal skins, or tapestries, your home becomes unclean and cluttered, which is not conducive to a spiritual people who may, from time to time, find themselves having to leave home with very little time to pack.

The human who succumbs to the perverse passion of hoarding has cleared a path straight to greed. What was once a useless clogging of clutter confined within your own tent becomes a destructive antisocial behavior poisoning the greater community. Soon your home is no longer ample space to closet your disordered piles of crap and you find yourself needing a second tent in which to store it.

Is owning a second tent forbidden in these commandments? No. But in having a second home, you have now planted the seeds of coveting in your neighbors' minds.

You may wonder why this should be your problem. The tenth commandment doesn't say you should do nothing to make your neighbors jealous. If your neighbors begin coveting what you own, is that your fault? Are you to blame if those with less than you fall into envy?

First of all, "fault" and "blame" are emotionally loaded terms—best avoided. We prefer "responsibility." And this is where it gets tricky. Not everyone among you will understand that your incessant need to acquire physical possessions is a sickness of the soul. Your more weak-minded neighbors will come to believe that your talent for gathering possessions is a virtue to be imitated.

The most perverse aspect of greed comes when two or more people under its influence join forces. Like a plague, the disease of greed spreads throughout the community and infects everyone. Once greed is allowed into your heart, everything that matters—love, empathy, compassion, and a sense of community—is eclipsed by an insatiable desire for more. Pretty soon your whole economic system is based on consuming.

Remember that it was your own greedy cousins who sold you into slavery. However you slice it, there is nothing good to say about greed. It's bad for the individual who succumbs to it and bad for the society that allows it. There is no room for greed. End of story.

Whatsoever you need to fulfill your destiny as a chosen people you have within you. Real *naches* does not come from excessive goods, money, power, or status. Focus on your mission and your lives will be filled with purpose and meaning.

You have been given all you need. What you have is enough. Tap into your inner strength, which comes from an invisible knowing faith in the ways of Heaven. Know that you will be fruitful and multiply. And if you prove yourselves especially worthy by impeccably keeping our covenant, many free lunches and all-expense-paid vacations await you.

18

Twelfth Commandment

Summary of Twelfth Commandment, Omitted by Moses:
Use your gifts as Heaven intended.

Children of Mother Earth's Humankind Project,

As with the last commandment, Moses kicked this commandment to the curb, saying it was too complicated for the Hebrews made simpleminded by multigenerational slavery. By this time, we had grown weary of all the back-and-forth over which of our commandments would make it into the final ten, so we placed this one on the shelf without argument.

Given your current state, it might be true that most of you are still too simpleminded to appreciate this commandment. Although you were long ago freed from physical slavery, your own conditioned likes and dislikes still keep you, metaphorically speaking, hogtied and hornswoggled. This is not a kosher state of mind.

Your own bodily urgings, wandering desires, and fleeting thoughts keep you imprisoned as if bound by invisible chains.

Even more sinister, while not as heavy as those of iron, these chains restrict you to an even greater extent because you are oblivious to how they continue to limit you. Our minions call your imaginary shackles the chain of fools. (We think that inspired another song.)

More puzzling still is that your species has forged these chains from the very divine gifts with which you were blessed. We gave you a body with which to joyfully use the physical capacities of sight, sound, touch, taste, smell, mobility, and stillness for the pleasure and benefit of all. Yet, rather than marshaling your body's resources in service to the common good, you hoard them for you own personal pleasure.

Beyond the reach of gross physical senses, we gave you the queen of all emotions: divine love. Revealing the vast invisible world of feelings as it does, divine love was designed as an inspiring sacred being impulse inclining you to treat everyone you encounter with kindness, compassion, forgiveness, and gratitude. And yet, rather than embracing everyone in your world with sympathetic warmth, you have diluted our gift into an exclusionary concern narrowly focused on you and yours only.

We gave you the sacred being impulse of faith to affirm your personal will with strength, courage, and divine guidance. This gift was to help you overcome all doubt with a simple knowing that, by aligning with divine will, you would be safe and protected. Strangely, you have debased faith into an endless sea of silly beliefs having nothing to do with the natural laws of Heaven and Mother Earth.

Even our gift of the sacred being impulse of hope has become empty, devoid of force. Hope puts into your own hands the means to accomplish whatever divine tasks you're guided to do. Hope is activated by your righteous service to your fellow humans through your own harmonious, lawful, skillful aspiring thoughts, trustworthy words, and engaged actions. But like waiting for the wind to answer your prayers, your hollowed out hope is but a passive wishing.

We gave you a thinking brain that enables you to help us manage Mother Earth's systems. Your thinking brain can observe, reason, correlate, critique, conceive, deduce, and imagine insightful conclusions. It can remember the planet's patterns, the better to plan your behaviors aligned with our natural laws. But instead, you most often use your thinking brain for making up stories to merely entertain, amuse, or scare yourselves.

The thinking brain's ability to conceive has been commandeered by your addictions to fear and escaping from reality. Your prefrontal cortex has been perverted into a masturbatory mechanism—ejaculating anxiety, uncertainty, and other useless imaginings.

As it has turned out, endowing humanity with the gift of creative thought was a damned if you do, damned if you don't proposition. In giving you the power to analyze and synthesize, we intended humanity to naturally step into its role as Heaven's cocreators on Mother Earth. Instead, you have each become so invested in your own unique perspective that most of you are obsessed with proving the rightness of your own point of view.

Let's spell it out for you: Your existence is about contributing your particular talents to help Mother Earth continue in her ability to sustain all of life, yours included. Showing off your own distinctive qualities that make you a unique individual was never the point. The divine gifts with which you were blessed were meant to make your life here on the planet useful to Heaven.

As a species, Homo sapiens has a collective destiny to fulfill as Heaven's cocreator. Likewise, each soul, by means of its natural endowments, has its own individual contribution toward achieving humanity's collective destiny. Ask not what Mother Earth can do for you, ask what you can do for Mother Earth.

19

Thirteenth Commandment

Summary of Thirteenth Commandment, Omitted by Moses: Thou shall pay attention.

Children of Mother Earth's Humankind Project,

In our experience, most humans have the attention span of a squirrel. This is because the thinking capacity of the average person is seldom stretched much beyond emotional desires and physical cravings. If your main concerns in life are obtaining food and mating, only a minimum of focus is necessary. It works out fine for squirrels. But being a member of a gaggle of tribes tasked with raising its own consciousness so it might help raise that of the rest of humanity requires more than the bare minimum amounts of attention needed for survival and procreation

If you *have* been paying attention, you will have noticed that a number of our commandments were designed to improve your memories, compromised as they have been by generations of acting as Egyptian pack animals and even more generations of acting as if you are *still* Egyptian pack animals. Yet what use is a keen memory if your awareness is so unfocused that it takes little into account worth remembering? The quality of your memory is in direct proportion to the quality of your attention.

Knowing Saint Moses as we do, even before presenting this commandment to him, we foresaw that he would object to its inclusion within the original agreed upon limit of ten. Without even bothering to read past our first paragraph, Moses declared it unnecessary. We understood that from his point of view, paying attention was so essential that devoting a whole commandment to it seemed superfluous. Keeping focused attention was an ability Moses took for granted.

In spite of our expectations for you to excel, none of you were raised with the advantages of Saint Moses. To assume that in your current state of stunted development you have the ability for sustained, collected attention is unrealistic, so we're starting from scratch.

Expanding your attention capacity requires bringing your physical, emotional, and thinking elements into simultaneous alignment. We're painfully aware that once again, thanks to Moses making this fundamental information "occult," most of you are unfamiliar with a state of expanded awareness. Had the general population been allowed access to the guide, we would all be far ahead of the game.

On rare occasions, your bodily sensations, feelings, and thoughts *can* spontaneously come into a state of alignment. You may have experienced such intermittent moments when your environment evoked them, say in times of urgent, life-and-death circumstances. But to actively live in such an ongoing awakened, heightened state of consciousness takes an ongoing dedication and perseverance of effort. Everyday, automatic, routine habits take over and you're lulled into a walking sleep.

Since you firmly believe that you're already awake, Heaven's challenge is convincing you to make the conscious effort needed to more fully awaken. This situation is ironic in and of itself, but add to that another irony. To conjoin these three major elements of your being takes—wait for it—attention. In other words, you need attention to grow attention. Life can be a bitch, especially if you're not paying attention.

To strengthen your attention means understanding it is not a purely intellectual effort. Notice yourself making concentrated efforts over a prolonged period while engaged with any task you enjoy. You're motivated in accomplishing the task through your pure enjoyment of it. The inherent interest in the task enhances your ability to stay focused with seemingly little or even no effort.

Now observe yourself making real efforts with a task you have no interest in and do not enjoy. Each passing minute might feel like an eternity—not that your limited perspective could ever grasp eternity, but you get our drift. Without enjoyment, the task weighs heavily. You find yourself resisting or even avoiding the task.

What is the lesson? Motivation fueled by pleasant emotion plays a key role in sustaining focused attention. Strengthening your attention comes down to maintaining a positive attitude in whatever task with which you are involved, even the less pleasant ones. From where does one derive this positive attitude? All one need do is go back to the first commandment: remembering us as creator and source.

In addition to the first commandment, you have also been given the gifts of the second and third commandments, designed for the very purpose of engendering even more gratitude. Receiving and keeping those commandments in the spirit of gratitude automatically strengthens your powers of attention.

The first commandment stresses that we took pity on you and freed you from a life of bondage. You were clueless slaves, chained to your physical bodies before we rescued you from a most miserable life. Keeping that commandment by putting us in your hearts and minds before all else is simply living in ongoing gratitude. How little we ask considering how you owe us, big time.

The second commandment, forbidding the making of any images you might be tempted to worship, serves as a further stretch of your attention. You are required to worship us as the invisible, untouchable spirit we are. You must conjure the feeling of gratitude and reverence without benefit of any physical representation of the sacred. In honoring what we have already done for you and showing us ongoing gratitude for what we continue to do for you from this time forward, your power of attention is further expanded.

But the most powerful exercise for building your atrophied attention muscles is contained within the third commandment. Unlike the first two, which are applicable at all times and in all places and circumstances, the third requires a more nuanced type of attention. One cannot rely on simple thoughtless habits.

Forbidding using our name in vain still allows its utterance for those times when saying our name is a good thing—making for a more intimate connection between us. Your selective attention must then be engaged to distinguish between which times are appropriate to say our name and which times are not.

This adds the element of discernment, which requires paying attention, and that is the point of this commandment.

When you pay attention to the gifts you have been given—your body, your emotions, your intellect—you see that the overall life we have given to you is beyond miraculous. Yours is a sacred existence. The task of awakening both yourselves and those around you is sacred. To fulfill it requires paying attention by staying in gratitude. You have the possibility of awakening to a freedom no physical chains can bind. Pay attention and don't blow it.

20

Fourteenth Commandment

Summary of Fourteenth Commandment, Omitted by Moses: Thou shall live in joy.

Children of Mother Earth's Humankind Project,

No way in hell was Saint Moses ever going to go for this commandment, which is arguably as important as any of the others. Ironically, if anybody needed to be joyous it was Mr. Pharaoh-in-waiting. Moses was something of a sourpuss and took himself way too seriously. The only time he smiled was when we cluelessly agreed he could have final editing rights to these commandments. What were we thinking? Negotiations, as we have mentioned, are not our strong suit. Just ask Beelzebub.

When it comes to achieving your mission, living in joy will get you to the top of a very steep mountain. While the goyim will no doubt be impressed with your success at fruiting and multiplying and your overall inherent cleverness, it is your unrelenting cheerfulness in the face of multiple adversities that will *really* have them scratching their heads. They might wonder what you're inhaling. People may even approach you about how to obtain some.

When we speak of living in joy, we're not speaking of simple happiness—though happiness is a decent enough place to start. Learning to appreciate the small things around you means paying attention, as already stressed in the previous lost commandment. But this commandment refers to real, irrepressible joy of being, which is not dependent on the pleasantries of external circumstance.

Admittedly, living in a permanent station of joy may seem a tall order, especially for a people traumatized after a dramatic escape from a life of oppression, tsuris, and *mishegas*. Fortunately, thanks to Heaven's clever design of the three divine gifts of intelligent awareness, there exists a quick and fairly easy way to transubstantiate trauma, hurt, or grief into at least a passable kind of happiness.

Dealing with trauma in the very moment it happens is, hands down, the best, most salubrious way to heal. But certain societal or time constraints often stop the needed drainage of trauma induced emotional pus. Maybe you were told that complaining is impolite or that boys should never cry. Perhaps you were running for your life from those bent on killing you. In such circumstances, who has the time or attention needed to heal from emotional wounds inflicted by trauma?

The pain of trauma unexpressed in the moment in which it happens stays lodged in the body, festering like an infected cut that has not been properly cleaned. Feelings of joy will seldom spontaneously manifest when obscured by untreated emotional hurts. The good news is that the accumulated pus of undischarged emotional wounding, no matter how long ago the wound was inflicted, can be adequately drained by reliving them in the present.

Be forewarned, though: Bringing feelings of past wounding into the present for purposes of discharging the unpleasant emotions connected with them is but a temporary cleansing remedy. Until you have understood the essence of real joy, you may find it necessary to repeat the discharge process around the same trauma many times. But given your current state, momentary joy is better than no joy at all.

To begin the proper discharging of clogged, festering emotion, you will need to feel safe. Discharging is often a messy, unsightly procedure and feelings of embarrassment can prevent the desired draining. In the beginning, you may try discharging while tending to your stock or pets. Assuming you don't have unnatural relations with them, these simple animals are unlikely to make you feel self-conscious during the discharge process.

Once you feel comfortable expressing old wounding among these creatures, the most powerful discharge is always produced in the presence of a sympathetic fellow human capable of giving you undivided, loving attention. You must then, as best you can, express whatever past trauma, anger, or grief that requires discharge.

To begin the process, you may find it necessary to tell your designated witness the details of the story surrounding your trauma. If you're doing a thorough enough job of explaining the trauma's origin, the emotions felt that went unexpressed will arise in you. Here is the important part: Let yourself act out, expressing these feelings as vividly as possible. To help get the tears rolling or the yelling or the screaming, we suggest pretending you're auditioning for a play.

Your acting out of these old, stuffed emotions might include quiet weeping, heavy sobbing, silly giggling, hysterical laughter, shaking, trembling, pillow punching, yelling, or even verbalizing naughty words at the top of your lungs. The more repressed among you might have to be satisfied with repeated yawning.

Whatever the case, you will not be a pretty sight, and it's therefore advised that your witness have the intestinal fortitude to continue watching with the aforementioned undivided, loving attention as you wail or thrash about with tears rolling down your cheeks or snot running out your nose.

Prior to throwing this tantrum, your sympathetic friend should know how long they're expected to witness it. Watching another in the throes of heavy emoting can be quite trying. The best strategy is to use a friend who desires a similar emotional healing for themselves and knows you are willing to witness them in turn. Splitting equal times as both witness and tantrum thrower is a convenient win-win.

The point is, you can, in just a few intentional moments, drain off gallons of emotional suffering by employing your body's instinctive capacity to heal wounds. And as stated, this doable but artificial method of discharging old, unresolved hurt is but a temporary substitute for living in the permanent station of genuine joy.

Real joy has no need for external dependency, coming as it does from your own Source of Powers within. Through gratitude, joy becomes spontaneous and sustained. And like joy itself, gratitude can be of a higher or lesser order. Real divine gratitude is available in the instant of recognizing the miraculousness of being.

Plain old common gratitude is merely the momentary overwhelm of appreciation after having received a gift. For instance, in addition to freeing you from slavery, Heaven has also bestowed multiple gifts upon you, and you are, or at least should be, feeling gratitude for them. Fair enough.

But the gratitude necessary for sustaining the permanent station of joy is what we speak of in this counsel. Gratitude is not a transitory appreciation for a gift *received* whose memory fades over time. Rather, the sacred being impulse of gratitude focuses on the overwhelm of awe from understanding that being able to *give* is a privilege.

Gratitude from receiving a gift is a sweet but diluted gratitude. Full strength gratitude, essential for self-generating joy, comes from performing kind, compassionate, selfless acts. Forgiveness is the most powerful of selfless acts, for there will be many times when forgiving seems impossible. Leaving the toilet seat up, however, should not be considered one of those times.

Selfless acts are the behaviors of cocreation. Your mission as a chosen people is fulfilled in such acts of selflessness. Heaven's burden is lightened whenever any human performs such an act. This is where the debt of your existence is paid. And if paying a debt for existing sounds harsh, wait until some religious organization comes along and tries to sell you the idea you were born in sin. That's a joy killer if ever there was one.

With all the "what if" logic arising in the lower, mechanical levels of your intellect, a nagging disbelief that forgiveness can always be given is understandable. "What if someone has wronged me, cheated me, or harmed my child? How am I supposed to recognize my privilege of being in service to such a person?" you ask.

Forgiveness is the simple answer. And as with Heaven's notion of creating a chosen people capable of raising the consciousness of all of humanity by raising its own, nothing was going to be simple. Perhaps you can now understand why so many of us were opposed to the chosen people idea. For now, just fake it 'til you make it.

Both real joy and real gratitude are sacred being impulses. Humanity's access to these two impulses comes through one of the three divine gifts of intelligent awareness. And if you were paying attention, you should know that these sacred being impulses were found inside the gift of emotional intelligence.

Now this is where it gets complicated, and you really do need to pay attention. Although we included forgiveness within emotional intelligence, it is *not*, strictly speaking, a sacred being impulse. In truth, it is more of an idea than a real emotion. In realizing that Homo sapiens would use any excuse, real or imagined, to avoid being in service to divine purpose, Heaven felt the necessity of hedging our bets, as it were, by including the intellectual concept of forgiveness inside the gift of emotional awareness.

Heaven's thinking was aimed at curtailing humanity's excuses that might prevent movement toward its destiny of being cocreators. Slipping the idea of forgiveness in with actual emotions was the best we could come up with on the fly. Without access to forgiveness, humans would be stuck in an endless cycle of anger, indignity, resentment, and revenge for every perceived hurt or grievance encountered, real or imagined.

Consider forgiveness a quasi-emotion, allowing the forgiver to move forward with his or her divine mission. From Heaven's perspective, there is nothing that *ever* needs forgiving. Would you have to forgive a scorpion for stinging you? Must you forgive a goat after it has chewed holes in your tent flap? Is forgiveness called for when your three-year-old-child wets its bed?

Any perceived wrong done to you is nothing but graceless behavior on the part of someone who has the consciousness of an unthinking creature or the self-control of a three-year-old. In *all* instances, the idea of forgiveness evaporates through compassionate understanding. Forgiveness lets both the perceived perpetrator and the perpetrated off the hook.

Though both the forgiven and the forgiver can move on with their lives, the forgiver is the major beneficiary. Holding on to a perceived hurt poisons the one who falsely believes in the reality of the hurt. Real forgiveness happens with the realization that there is nothing to forgive.

And while we're on the topic of quasi-emotions, we feel compelled to address the destructive energy of guilt. Like forgiveness, guilt is not a *real* emotion either. But unlike Heaven-conceived forgiveness, guilt is but a totally *false* emotion created by a lazy humanity perverting the noble sacred being impulse remorse of conscience.

Heaven included remorse of conscience in its gift of emotional intelligence as an extra precaution to smooth the often rocky road to forgiveness. When the perceived perpetrator feels remorse of conscience, they are compelled to make amends for what they have done to the injured party.

The act of forgiving is made that much easier for the injured party when the perceived perpetrator makes amends for the perceived perpetration. This assumes, of course, that the forgiver has not yet cultivated compassionate understanding and is therefore not yet hip to the fact that nothing ever really needs forgiving.

The false emotion of guilt requires nothing more of the perpetrator than just feeling bad. No amends are required, and the perpetrator is free to continue perpetrating. Both "victim" and "victimizer" are imprisoned in negative emotions—the victim by not forgiving and the victimizer by feelings of guilt. Joy has left the building.

The tools of gratitude and forgiveness may help you rise above feelings of victimhood and revenge, but at its most basic, joy is a celebration of life—your life—the only one you have. Start celebrating your life by loving yourself. We are not speaking of indulgent pleasure seeking but rather loving yourself by taking care of yourself. Know what activities you love and what people you love. Make time for doing those activities and hanging out with those people. Joy is waiting in the wings.

21

Fifteenth Commandment

The, For Real, Fourteenth Dalai Lama's Version: Be kind whenever possible. It is always possible.

Children of Mother Earth's Humankind Project,

We could not have expressed the sentiments of this commandment better than the Fourteenth Dalai Lama (one of our messengers, BTW). We certainly could not have said it shorter. As with our lack of negotiation skills, so it is with the skill at brevity. Saint Moses himself would have been impressed had he possessed the courage to face his demons. What else could have caused Moses to reject this most obvious of all our commandments? If one were always kind, there would be little need for most of the other commandments.

Like the previous four lost commandments, Saint Moses used his veto power to prevent most people from ever seeing our fifteenth commandment. In not having broader access to this particular commandment, humanity is now living with the catastrophic consequences. The modern State of Israel's most recent brutal behavior toward its colonized indigenous population has served only to intensify humanity's myriad other existential crises. Our once so-called "chosen people" continue making very bad choices.

Having learned nothing after their millennia of abuse by others, the Israelis have now become abusers. This is the opposite of Heaven's intention for creating chosen people in the first place. And as chronicled earlier, Heaven was quite aware it was opening a can of worms in taking such drastic action.

More so than the other four lost commandments Moses rejected, this particular one was, to say the least, his most emphatic veto. Based on the level of his reactivity, we suspected we had hit a raw nerve. But by then, after all the niggling back and forth editing of the commandments and discussions about which commandments would or would not be included in the final ten, we were feeling drained.

While Saint Moses certainly had his virtues, kindness was not one of them. As you may recall, in his youth, Moses led Pharaoh's army into battle after battle, leaving piles of dead bodies in his wake. We could go on recounting how Moses bristled at the very notion of kindness being a requirement of Heaven, but that in itself would be less than kind—not at all in keeping with the theme of this commandment.

It should be said that before finally bestowing sainthood on Moses for his success in leading the Hebrews out of Egypt, a controversy almost as big as creating a chosen people broke out in Heaven. Our minions reached consensus on the matter only after days of debate. With all that blood on his hands, you may have wondered how we ever rationalized giving such a noble honor to one so brutal as Moses. Chalk it up to sentimentality and the fact that it was just an honorary title anyway. And we were following our own advisement to be kind whenever possible.

You might think that being kind is second nature for a species that refers to itself as "humankind." After all, Heaven stuffed your DNA with quite a few cooperative genes, instincts for empathy, and sacred being impulses like love, compassion, and humility—not to mention kindness itself.

As with a number of other fail-safes built into the Humankind Project, Heaven underestimated gravity's crushing power to thwart them within three-dimensional reality. At this point, the best thing we can do is lay out what we mean by "kindness" and hope you will take its essential nature to heart—which is exactly that part of you where kindness resides.

Kindness is often confused with charity. And while charity may result from an act of kindness, it ain't necessarily so. A charitable act may be performed simply because of other people's perceptions of you. Charity may well be an act of vanity, as noted troubadour, Bob Dylan, proclaims in "Ballad of a Thin Man." We'll leave it to you to decipher how the lyrics to that song address our meaning.

Kindness is not transactional and not about convenience. Kindness is a way of being, not a display of occasional behavior when you feel like it or when you're expecting something in return. Being kind will *often* be inconvenient. But no matter what the circumstances, one always has the capacity to be kind. You may find it easier to always be kind by remembering that everyone you meet is struggling with the same powerful denying force of the three-dimensional reality with which you struggle.

As it is with the difficulty of living from joy, so is it with always being kind. You're going to meet people whose behavior will evoke distain or anger in you. Those are the very people for whom you need to cultivate an unshakable kindness. Start with yourself—the person for whom offering kindness is often most difficult.

Cultivating kindness, both for yourself and all others, starts with genuine humility fostered by a deep knowing that in a contest of schmucks, you are such a schmuck that you wouldn't make it to schmuck number three. So be gentle on yourself and take heart in the fact that you're not even in the running for biggest schmuck in the world.

While this may sound harsh and not at all kind, particularly in light of this commandment, please realize that after watching your species for lo these many years, it is a conclusion based on solid empirical evidence—underscored by the world's unceasing wars.

Kindness begets kindness, having the power to bring people together. Israel's mission as a chosen people could have succeeded had it learned kindness. The gaps that have prevented it from working harmoniously with others could have been bridged.

How bitter are these words as we have watched the modern State of Israel position itself as an agent representative for the Western powers vying for a toehold on the energy rich region of the Middle East. Perhaps we should have gone along with Archangel Meshuggah's suggestion of placing the promised land in Utah.

Why a chosen people, indeed? Who are we kidding? Talk about Heaven's monumental goof! As explained above, we kind of knew we were wasting our breath when this commandment was first given to Moses. Little did we realize that a goodly number of Hebrews felt a similar antipathy for kindness. The brutal behavior of modern Israel has now born this out.

In its brazen ethnic cleansing toward its colonized indigenous population, Israel has repudiated its divine mission to teach humanity about becoming Heaven's cocreators.

As explained earlier, the Hebrews were not our first choice. Not that our original pick, the Babylonians, would have done any better. But we doubt it would have taken nearly six millennia to find out.

Still, the original mistake is knocking on Heaven's door. So just for the record, we are *so* over the chosen people thing. Be advised that our near six-thousand-year-old covenant with the descendants of Abraham, Isaac, and Jacob is now officially dissolved. Kindness, schmindness.

Afterword

by Supreme Archangel Beelzebub

HEAVEN'S RECENTLY REGAINED CELEBRATORY ATMOSPHERE will not be impacted by whether or not Mother Earth's human population awakens to its divine destiny. While there has been no official pronouncement, SOP has stopped denying its Humankind Project may be failing. This isn't to say that Heaven has stopped cheering for you. We still consider Mother Earth to be humanity's home venue, but nothing is forever, and there are other luscious planets right here in this galaxy.

Our own hope is that through your ongoing experience with the results of planetary-wide plagues, bad political choices, and total identification with your separate selves, you are arriving at one of those famous teachable moments. Many of you do seem ready to reflect on your own contributions to your many conundrums. The question becomes this: With the little time you have left, are there enough of you to change humanity's tragic trajectory, a trajectory which, sad to say, no amount of shopping with your up-cycled cloth bags made from old REI backpacks is going to change?

You've probably figured out by now that SOP isn't as infallible as its press would have you believe. SOP should have consulted with me way before things went so south for you. But SOP was understandably gun-shy regarding my advice and never gave me the chance to offer my two cents until now—at the bottom of humanity's ninth inning.

If SOP hadn't asked for my editorial help, this book would be the latest failed effort to reinvigorate humanity's languishing upward evolutionary impulse. When SOP showed me an early draft, I almost plotzed. Between the bad puns and overly earnest attitude, SOP would have been lucky to get three of you to read it.

When it comes to wordsmithery, you might wonder why SOP called on me instead of Gabriel. After all, Gabriel *is* the archangel of communication. No doubt SOP knew that more serious help was needed at humanity's critical hour and had the good sense to know that using another yes-man archangel wasn't going to cut it.

And there is no more serious help to be found to coauthor than yours truly, SOP's original cocreator. Perhaps you've noticed the apparent dualistic nature of your physical reality? Up, down? Out, in? Hot, cold? Well half of that reality falls to my department.

Does the Bible even once mention the fact that SOP could not have actualized the necessary ingredients for creation without my contributions? At the risk of shocking you, SOP didn't make the firmament, the seas, or the creepy-crawlies swimming in them all by itself. All of creation was pretty much a fifty-fifty deal.

Consider the firmament upon which you now stand. You'd be floating in space without my void. Consider also the light of illumination. Good luck seeing any without my dark matter. Do you think it's a coincidence I'm sometimes known as the Prince of Darkness?

And as long as we're giving the devil his due, I hereby acknowledge SOP's courage in asking for my help on this project. SOP had to swallow several fleets of cargo ships full of pride knowing full well I'd be giving it one of my famous tongue-lashings.

True enough. After reading SOP's early draft of this volume, I unloaded on SOP harder than John Henry's hammer. My immediate reaction was, "Forget those losers down there! Cut your losses and get something going with one of those other planets on which you've been wanting to spread your seed."

But then it struck me: Maybe this perfect storm of catastrophes which humanity has largely brought upon itself was an opening to clarity. What if its latest pandemic reveals the prevailing poor health of the world's population? What if Earth's collapsing ecological systems are spurring governments and corporations to funnel their giant investments away from burning fossil fuels?

What if humanity's failing supply chains encouraged addicted consumers to question their compulsive consumption? What if the current worldwide political flirtations with fascism sent Hitler-flavored nightmares shivering down humanity's collective spine? What if the thousand years of hostility between Israel and its Arab neighbors scares everyone enough to prevent a third world war?

Better yet, what if Heaven admitted to its colossal goofs in creating a chosen people, making gravity too sticky, and being too ready to let Moses have final edits? What if Heaven's monumental errors were shown to be even more monumental by revealing its shortsighted promise, giving a rather dubious chosen people its own nation smack in the middle of the most highly contested land on the planet?

Appropriate for simple fight-or-flight decisions, fear has long been the great motivator for focusing humanity's attention. But let's face it, fear stimulates the older, most habituated part of the brain, which is ill-equipped for unraveling complexity. Heaven blessed Homo sapiens, Mother Earth's newest species, with the gifts of newer brain parts. As a result, humanity has the ability to obtain a nuanced understanding of its existence available to no other species.

The bad news—as humanity's desperate situation points to so vividly—is that humans are prone to forget they have the ability for nuanced understanding. But the good news is that those newer parts of the brain containing higher thinking capacities are also where humanity's sense of humor delicately dangles. The ability to laugh at yourself can be an even greater motivator than fear.

Your ignorant, self-obsessed behavior magically becomes less ignorant and less self-obsessed when you're forced to laugh at the absurdity of a self-created situation. This is the very reason Heaven started giving its would-be messengers the option to incarnate as comedians.

So perhaps here is where humanity's perfect storm of doom and gloom is inexorably blown away by peals of laughter. Maybe here, in revealing that even exalted Heaven makes mistakes and is willing to own its foibles, humanity—especially of the male variety—is willing to do the same. And in that willingness, perhaps it will stop its own ignorant behavior. (A personal note: Based on my many years observing humans, it appears that most ignorant behavior is made from the *his* gender side of the spectrum. Four thousand years of patriarchy is bound to skew statistics.)

There's no denying that a few of Heaven's questionable managerial decisions with the Humankind Project have run counter to its original plans for humanity's divine destiny. Of course, none of our stupid decisions compare to the human invention of planned obsolescence. But then, humanity *is* only human.

Allowing yourself to grasp the terror of your situation will prove a big help in finding the truest path out of the woods. Not that you should be leaving the woods altogether. You'd be so much better off today if you had preserved your gratitude for Mother Earth's biodiversity. What are you thinking, cutting down Mother Earth's rainforests—the very lungs of the planet—as if they were metastasizing organs? And for what? To more easily graze cattle so you can continue making cheap, really bad hamburgers?

Allow me to apologize if my anger is putting off any potential readership that might help spread the word about revivifying humanity's divine destiny as cocreators. Righteous indignation is never a good look on anybody. So I completely understand if you wish to avoid any further challenges to your sensibilities.

Believe me, I won't be offended if you decide this book was a waste of your time, forget everything we've been discussing here, and go back to reading *Consumer Reports* or *Sports Illustrated*. But before you go off to google that bikini-clad beach beauty or compare which air fryer is the best value, please know that all your pain arises from not engaging with the upward evolutionary impulse.

Surrendering to the downward impulse has handed you a life sentence inside a prison of your own making. You've built walls around yourselves using the bricks, rocks, and cement of habitual thoughts, egotistic feelings, and mechanical actions. That you are able to move about from one cell to another, paint the walls with designer colors, or install wall-to-wall carpeting does not set you free.

So in keeping with that prison metaphor, think of this book as a kind of pickax for tunneling under your self-created prison. Should you grab it by the handle and swing it enough times with sufficient strength, you might dig a narrow passage of possible escape. And narrow though it may be, the very effort of digging can shed enough poundage that, with a generous application of sustainably sourced coconut butter, you might conceivably slither to freedom.

Or for those of you finding tunneling too claustrophobic, think of this book as your own personal set of wings which, by flapping them very hard, glides you up and over the wall. Of course, accomplishing such a feat assumes your willingness to discard the considerable physical, emotional, and conceptual baggage increasing gravity's already too sticky force on you.

Everyone up here is crossing their fingers, praying that humanity's long awaited great awakening may finally be happening. Yet, even with this potential planetwide opening at hand, not even SOP, this universe's version of Supreme Being, knows its outcome. Our hope is that enough of you will use the tools found in this volume to alter humanity's current trajectory.

Should this book's purpose begin to have any affect at all, we will begin sensing a revivifying of the upward evolutionary impulse emanating from Mother Earth. By the same token, you may begin noticing certain restorations in Mother Earth's interdependent biological systems. "Stay balanced" will suddenly become the in phrase of the moment, much as "far out" was to some of you, decades ago.

But what kind of hard teller of truth would I be, ending on such an up note? If not for SOP's overly sentimental attachment to your sorry-ass species, I'd have insisted on finding a worthier bunch of souls eager to make the conscious labors and intentional sufferings required to transubstantiate your lower natures into being presence.

Perhaps it's time to dust off Archangel Schmoozer's old report, "Termites: Master Builders of Sustainability." But then, what kind of cocreator would I be if I'd refused to help my oldest and best friend? Oh, and BTW, SOP is also expecting help from its creation as well. Hope you can take a hint. You would be wise to get your tuches in gear and give it your all.

Acknowledgments

EVERYONE IS A POTENTIAL TEACHER, and had I been paying better attention, this book would be all the better off for it. However, I did have the good fortune to meet quite a number of individuals, both directly and indirectly, whose lessons were not to be ignored. So I wish to thank those who contributed to this book, both knowingly and unknowingly.

Had COVID-19 not arrived on the scene, whether from an accidental laboratory leak or unnatural human-to-bat intimacy, the writing of this book would likely still be in doubt. The pandemic's lockdown did much to keep me focused on this project.

That being said, being forced to stay at home would not have been near enough inspiration had not my author-wife, Susan Guyette, been there with me the whole time. Watching her finish her own manuscript, followed by a big-time publisher snapping it up just three weeks after submission, oxygenated my flickering creative candle into the steady flame needed for my own task.

Those of you familiar with the unfathomable great work left by G.I. Gurdjieff will recognize his influence on this book's formation. Had he not written *Beelzebub's Tales to His Grandson*, this book, likewise, would not have been written. Forget about thinking outside the box. Gurdjieff granted permission to think outside the solar system.

Tremendous encouragement came at a crucial time from James Levinson's gracious reading of an early draft of this man-uscript. Much thanks to James for recognizing and contributing to this book's spirit of fun without once mentioning its tedium.

I am blessed to have found the experienced and delicate editor, Melanie Mulhall, who teased and squeezed out the tedium, punched up the clarity, and turned me on to Veronica Yager of Journey Bound Publishing, whose book design skills are obvious for all to see.

Big thanks also go out to my super encouraging friends, Eduardo Krasilovsky, Sanjiv Manifest, and David Leach. Eduardo told me this book was important and I should get it published. Sanjiv thought the whole concept hysterical and was splitting his guts before ever reading a word of it. David, for whom the term "tough audience" was coined, admitted that in glancing at a few chapters, he laughed out loud.

Please indulge the mention of my son, Ezra Sage, who fills me with awe. Not yet thirty, still just shy of his official Saturn return, Ezra epitomizes a grown up, responsible adult who has made it his business to live a creative, vital life in service to both himself and his community.

And finally, how can I not thank my own lucky stars, aligning me with the privilege of indulging my quirky self-expression beyond an idle hobby? I mean, can it be idle if you're seriously intending to tickle someone's funny bones while at the same time getting them to hiccup?

About the Author

GERSHON SIEGEL WROTE *The Ten Commandments Reboot* in the hope of liberating as many souls as possible without his having to take the Bodhisattva vow. He is also the author of *Paradigms Lost: Online Oracles for the New Millennium*, a satirical take on the dangers of hard, fast, literal beliefs proffered by the New Age, the Old Age, or any age for that matter.

Siegel's writing career began at Steubenville High School (Steubenville, Ohio) when his journalism teacher, fresh out of college, made him feature editor of the school newspaper. Perhaps she failed to smell the danger in doing so or perhaps she simply intuited it was time for that sleepy little Ohio Valley town to hear from its disaffected youth, thus explaining why she continued to allow Siegel to write a humor column for most of his senior year—right up until the school's principal decided enough was enough. Either way, that journalism teacher was the first but not the last, to support Gershon as a smarty-pants writer.

Siegel's writing career includes a stint as editor and columnist for *Santa Fe Spirit* and twelve-year run as a Santa Fe based publisher, editor, columnist, and reporter for *Sun*

Monthly, a well received magazine of personal, practical, and planetary concerns.

Rumor has it that Gershon moved to Santa Fe in the summer of 1981 because the May cover headline of *Esquire Magazine* proclaimed, "Yes, There Is One Last Place to Go." Ten years later Siegel migrated to a semi-rural part of Santa Fe County where he and his wife, Susan Guyette, enjoy working on their books and feeling grateful for the mountain vistas offered by the heartland of Southwest suburbia.

www.ingramcontent.com/pod-product-compliance
Lightning Source LLC
Chambersburg PA
CBHW072134300726

48975CB00003B/1066